Dr. R. Koch

Aetiology of Tuberculosis

Dr. R. Koch

Aetiology of Tuberculosis

ISBN/EAN: 9783742832979

Manufactured in Europe, USA, Canada, Australia, Japa

Cover: Foto ©Andreas Hilbeck / pixelio.de

Manufactured and distributed by brebook publishing software
(www.brebook.com)

Dr. R. Koch

Aetiology of Tuberculosis

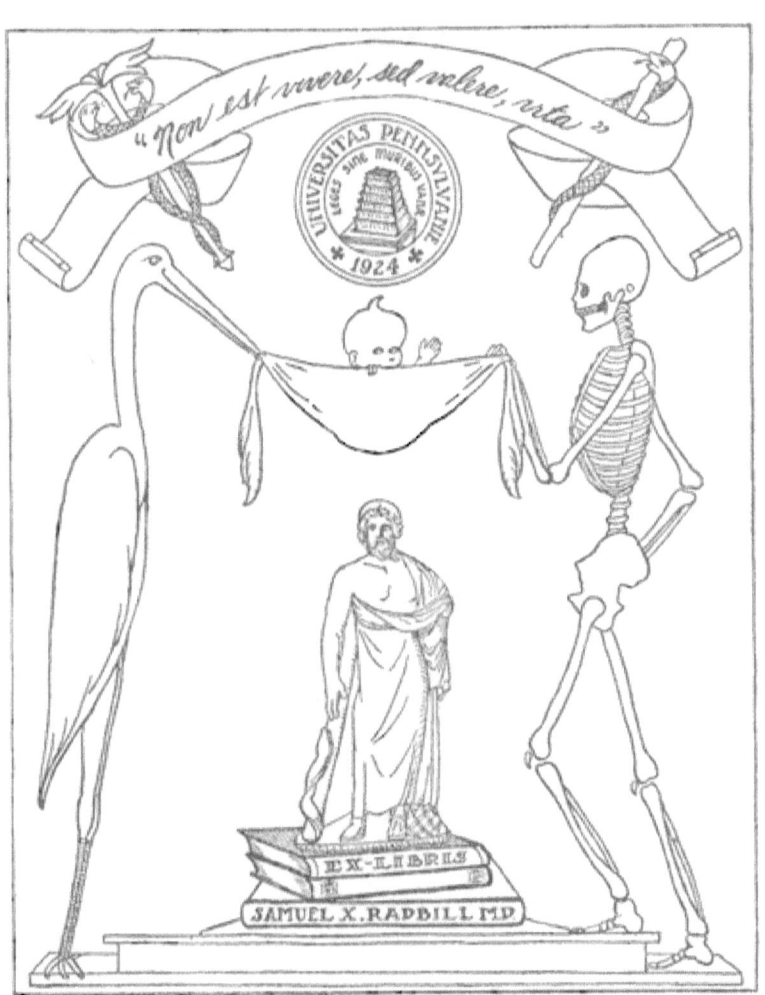

ÆTIOLOGY

OF

TUBERCULOSIS

BY

Dr. R. KOCH,

Privy Council.

—

Translated by Rev. T. SAURE.

Transactions of the Massachusetts Veterinary Medical-Association.

Reprinted from the *American Veterinary Review.*

New York:
WILLIAM R. JENKINS,
Veterinary Publisher and Bookseller,
851 & 853 Sixth Avenue.
—
1890.

PREFACE.

Dr. Koch's treatise on the Ætiology of Tubercolosis, has been translated with the authorization of the author, and is presented to the medical and veterinary professions of the United States as the most remarkable work on the subject. It is reprinted from the American Veterinary Review, and the translation is due to the Massachusetts State Veterinary Medical Association, who recognized its importance and undertook the labor of the work. The present edition is due to the demand for the treatise in its entirety, and although it is issued without the illustrations of the costly German edition, it will be found of the greatest advantage to all investigations in the subject.

That the bacillus of Koch is the cause of tubercular disease; that to these are due all the different lesions of the various tissues in which it is found implanted ; and that it is then invariably present, though, perhaps at times, difficult to discover, to color, or to isolate; and that, unless it is *there*, tuberculosis DOES NOT EXIST—all this is proved beyond question or doubt in Koch's " Ætiology." The modes of development, the processes of the biological studies which are required for the investigation ; everything discoverable, in fact, connected with this bacillus, are minutely, carefully, and thoroughly described and presented by the author to the inquiring student. With this work properly appreciated and well studied, there is no longer any reason for error of diagnosis in that fatal affection. The lesions are in many instances so characteristic that any error can scarcely be possible, and yet how frequently may it happen that lesions, of the lungs, for instance, often peculiar, may be of a tuberculous aspect and yet entirely different in their nature ! The pseudo-tubercules of the lungs, sometimes encountered, have no doubt in some instances led to a diagnosis of alleged phthisis, which would have been of an entirely different nature had the teachings of the author been followed, and the truth discerned, which the absence of the bacilli would have made certain, if it had but been rightly interpreted.

" Ætiology of tuberculosis," which has filled so important a place among German scientific authorities, may now perform the same good office for English-speaking veterinarians, and by such of us as may unfortunately have much to do with this disease in the United States, we hope it will be recognized as an instructor and assistant beyond any possibility of rivalry or cavil, or chance of supercedure.

ÆTIOLOGY OF TUBERCULOSIS.

A series of investigations of the Ætiology of Tuberculosis which I have been making within the last few years have led me to results which were first reported before the Physiological Society of Berlin, March 24th, 1882 (Berliner klinische Wochenschrift, 1882, No. 15). My communications at that time, however, could only embrace the most important points, while the more minute description of the attempts was necessarily reserved for a detailed report. Since then, by continued investigations, many gaps have been filled and new matter added. The report of my labors in the investigation of the ætiology of tuberculosis, completed and enlarged by these researches, is given in the following.

The question whether tuberculosis is a disease dependent upon transmitted disease-germs can be approached in different ways, as this has in fact been done. It has been attempted to secure certainty, partly with the aid of clinical observations, partly by means of anatomical and also by experimental investigations. Most uncertain are the results of the experience gathered at the sickbed. It is true, cases occur in the experience of every physician with fair practice, in which he cannot fail to see a transmission of tuberculosis from one person to another. Then, however, follow numerous cases in which every possibility of infection seems to be excluded. Attempts have been made repeatedly to prove the contagious nature of phthisis, but they must be looked upon as failures, as such views have never found acceptance among scientists. Some clinical authorities, to be sure, have not lost view of the possibility of contagion, but on the whole physicians consider phthisis a non-contagious disease, proceeding from constitutional anomalies. An indication of the infectious character of tuberculosis, which cannot be ignored, was given by pathological anatomy, when Buhl called attention to the connection of miliary tuberculosis with käse-herden,* (a German technical term of which I do not know the meaning in the English language) and offered the proposition that general tuberculosis is to be looked upon as a disease which is brought about by the resorption of a virus present in the primary käse-herd (cheesy-nodule), hence as it were, by auto-infection. As to the manner in which tuberculous virus spreads itself through the body, the discoveries of Ponfick in regard to the thoracic duct and of Weigert in regard to veinous tubercles in miliary tuberculosis have given light. However, these facts only prove the spread of tuberculous virus in the body itself, without proving the transmission from one individual to another, in which latter the contagious nature really consists. With this last question experimental pathology has occupied itself in the most searching manner. The course taken in experimental investigations of the infectious nature of tuberculosis has been described of late very minutely, (cf, Johne, Die Geschichte der Tuberculose. Leipzig, 1883), so that I can omit the historical details and confine myself to a few remarks on the more important heads.

---

*Cheesy nodules.—S.

Solitary, incomplete and negative attempts to generate tuberculosis artificially were made towards the end of the last century. The first successful attempts were made by Klencke, who by inoculation of miliary and infiltrated tubercles from the human being into the cervical veins of rabbits, brought about a widespread tuberculosis of the lungs and liver. Klencke must therefore be pronounced the discoverer of experimental tuberculosis. He did not continue his attempts, and so they were almost forgotten. In a systematic and thorough manner experimental tuberculosis was worked out by Villemin. He not only inoculated tuberculous substances from the human subject, but also from the pearl disease of cattle, and showed by experiment the identity of pearl disease and tuberculosis. Villemin's investigations seemed already, by the number of experiments, by their careful execution and comparison with opposing attempts bearing upon the same question, to have decided the question in favor of the infection theory. Nevertheless the numerous investigators who repeated Villemin's attempts according to the methods suggested by him or in modified ways, arrived at very contradictory results. The defenders of the infection theory, especially Klebs, sought to improve the experimental technique and to free it from the errors clinging to it; the opponents, on the contrary, strove to prove that the tuberculous substance possessed no virulent properties, and true tuberculosis could be produced by inoculation with material in which tuberculosis did not exist. This dispute was first settled by the experiments of Cohnheim and Salomonsen who, with this end in view, inoculated the anterior chamber of the eyes of rabbits. It was an exceedingly happy idea to make use of the rabbit eye as the place of inoculation. From the nature of the case, those cases in which tuberculous substance only has been inoculated must be distinguished from those in which other infectious material has been combined with the tuberculous virus. In subcutaneous inoculation, such materials often produce more or less widespread caseous infiltrations, which are not unlike the tuberculous cheesy products. In the eye, on the contrary, they cause an inflammation which rapidly runs its course, which can in no case be mistaken for the inoculated tuberculosis, which is slow and unique in its development. This inoculated tuberculosis, when the experiment is successful, takes such a course that it is always manifest to the investigator. After a somewhat prolonged stage of incubation little gray nodules appear in the iris, scarcely visible to the naked eye and proceeding from the transplanted portions of tuberculous substance. The number of these nodules increases gradually, they themselves grow, become yellowish in the center, become cheesy and show as well macroscopically as microscopically all the typical characteristics of genuine tuberculous nodules.

Tuberculous infection is, moreover, not confined to the eye, but spreads itself later through the entire organism; it attacks especially the neighboring lymphatic glands, the lungs, spleen, liver and kidneys. According to the united testimony of Cohnheim and Salomonsen and all other experimenters, who have repeated these attempts, an iris-tuberculosis has in no case followed the inoculation with non-tuberculous substances. More than this, a spontaneous case of iris-tuberculosis in rabbits has never been observed. This method of infection is therefore superior to all others in so far as that the influence of unintentional errors in attempt is shut out, errors which so easily creep into the experiments in subcutaneous inoculation and in transplantation into the abdominal cavity. The chance of mistaking artificial tuberculosis for that arising spontaneously **is also** completely excluded. Therefore in comparing the attempts of Cohnheim and Salomonsen with those previously **made**, they must be admitted to be completely free from objection, and by them it is proved that the most different **tuberculous substances** contain a specific and individual element.

Of what character this infectious matter **might be, whether it be formed by** means of organisms independent, **or provided with unvarying properties, which** force themselves into the body as parasites and communicate tuberculosis to **it, or** whether the infectious material exists only in **certain conditions of the body and** consists of organized or unorganized formations arising from **its own ingredients,** was a question that for the time being could **not** be decided. **But after the results,** which have been attained **of late years regarding the ætiology of** many infectious diseases, the possibility that also the cause of tuberculosis was to be sought in some sort of micro-organisms, seems to be indicated. **In order to obtain light on** this point, it was necessary to make use of all that experience which had proved itself useful in the examination of other infectious diseases, **and the same course** of investigation was to be chosen which in other cases had shown itself most to the purpose. To make the best use of these advantages, the attempts were to be made in the following manner: In the first place, it must be **decided whether form** elements, not belonging to the elements of the **body, or arising from them, are** present **in the diseased parts.** If the existence of **such can be proved, then we** must investigate whether the same be organized and whether they **offer any signs** of independent life, among which independent motion, (for which **molecular mo-** tion is very often mistaken), growth, increase and generation are **to be reckoned.** Further, the relations to their surroundings, **the** conduct of **the** components **of** the neighboring textures, their diffusion in the body, their appearance at **the va-** rious stages of the disease, and other **circumstances** must be traced, **which, with** more or less probability, **show a primary connection** between these **formations** and the disease. **It is possible that the facts gained in** this manner **may afford** such proof that only the most extreme scepticism can maintain that micro-organ- isms found are no cause, but only an accompaniment of the disease. Often, of course, this objection is justified, and therefore it is necessary for a complete system of proof that one should not confine himself to showing the co-existence **of** the disease and **parasites**, but that, more than this, these parasites must be shown to be the real cause of the disease. **This can only be done by removing** the parasites from the diseased organism completely, and freeing them from all products of the disease to which a hurtful influence **could be ascribed, and that** by the introduction of the isolated parasites into **the healthy organism, the dis-** ease with all its peculiar characteristics should be **produced anew. An example** **may serve to explain** what has **just** been said. **If the blood of animals which** have died from inflammation **of the spleen be** examined, **there are always** found therein numerous minute, **rod-shaped, colorless,** motionless **forms. One** could not see immediately that these **minute rods are of** a vegetable nature, and indeed in the beginning they **were often held for lifeless** crystalline bodies. First from the circumstance that they were seen **to grow from** spores, and that from **the** spores little rods **were developed anew, could it be** decided with certainty **that** they possessed life **and belonged to the lowest class of plants.** Further,

when the very smallest amount of the blood of an animal dying of inflammation of the spleen is inoculated into another animal, said animal invariably
dies of the same disease, and it also contains the little rods, the so-called "bacilli"
of inflammation of the spleen. This does not prove, however, that by the
inoculation of the little wands, the disease was communicated. In order to know
whether the bacilli, and not other components of the blood of inflammation
of the spleen, produces said inflammation, the bacilli must be separated from the
blood, and be inoculated alone.

The isolation of the bacilli can be ascertained with most certainty by continued cultivation apart from all other things. To this end, a small quantity of
blood containing bacilli is placed upon some fixed nutrient soil, on which the
bacilli are able to grow, for instance, nutrient gelatine or boiled potatoes. Here
they soon begin to increase very rapidly, while the other components of the blood,
corpuscles and serum, remain unchanged. After two or three days, when the
bacilli have formed a dense mass of spore-holding threads, the smallest possible
of the no longer blood-red, but whitish looking mass, is taken and again placed
upon nutrient gelatine or boiled potatoes. The bacilli increase in exactly the
same manner as in the first planting, and form a dense white mass on the potato,
and already in this second transplanting the most careful examination with the
microscope will scarcely show any traces of the other components of the blood.
In like manner the continued transplanting is carried on. After the third or
fourth, the bacilli may be considered free from all other parts of the blood, which
at first were planted with them. If the transplantations now are repeated twenty
or fifty times, or still oftener, then it may be concluded with all imaginable certainty, that not the least taint of the disease clings to the bacilli. Even inter-
nally they could hide nothing of that kind; for the finest planted bacilli are also
no longer present, and their descendants for many generations have obtained the
necessary material for their growth from their fostering soil, the potato. The
pure breed obtained in this way has no connection with the diseased organism
from whose blood the first planting came, and with the products of disease, which
belong to animal metamorphosis. Nevertheless, as soon as they are inoculated
into a healthy animal, they produce the fatal disease. The inoculated animal
sickens as quickly and with the same symptoms as if it had been inoculated with
blood fresh from a diseased animal, or had spontaneously become diseased with
inflammation of the spleen, and in its blood appear the same innumerable
bacilli as in the natural disease, which have the same properties as the well known
bacilli of inflammation of the spleen. In view of these facts, there is no
other explanation, than that said bacilli are not an accompaniment of inflammation of the spleen, but the real cause of this disease. Now inflammation
of the spleen does not always present the same clinical appearance; its form
varies in the different species of animals; in the case of man it can run its
course with the symptoms of a general infection, without prominent local disturbances, or it can remain purely local and confine itself to a certain point on
the outer skin, on the gut, or on the larynx. Nevertheless also in these cases, if
the characteristic bacilli are found in the diseased places, we must consider them
as the cause of the disease; for their disease-producing qualities are known to
us, and we cannot very well imagine that in the tissues of the same organism the

bacilli are at one time harmless, at another time disease-producing parasites. These conclusions are so indisputable that probably nobody questions them, and that in science the bacilli of inflammation of the spleen are considered the cause as well of the usual typical disease as appearing in our domestic animals, as also of the clinically varying type which appears in man.

The course just sketched, which those who strove to prove the parasitic nature of inflammation of the spleen have taken with success, and the conclusions necessarily obtained from the results, I have placed at the foundation of my investigation of the ætiology of tuberculosis. These had to employ themselves in the first place with the proof of disease-producing organisms, then with their isolation, then with their inoculation. I now go over to the description of these single divisions of the investigation.

I.—*Proof of the presence of disease-producing organisms in the organs changed by tuberculosis and in the separation of the latter.*

Disease-producing organisms, which have the size of inflammation-of-the-spleen bacilli and like these, appear in the blood in large numbers, or those which, like the "nekurrensperochaeten" attract the eye, offer no especial difficulties in investigation, and the proof of such micro-organisms can be obtained by ordinary optical helps. The case is different, however, when it is necessary to prove the existence of minute bacteria present in the tissues in only small numbers, especially when cells are heaped up or broken down in the spots concerned, which is almost always the case. Then it is necessary to use the more delicate technical helps of microscopy, as especial methods of preparation and differential coloring, and to pursue the investigations with the best optical apparatus, oil-immersion systems and Abbe's illuminating apparatus.

Also in regard to tuberculosis it was to be expected that to show that special disease-producing organisms do actually exist, might offer special difficulties, as they had already been much sought for, and nothing found that could give confidence in their existence. I began investigations with material in which infectious matter might be expected with certainty, for instance, in freshly developed and still grey tubercles from the lungs of animals which had been killed three or four weeks after inoculation. From these lungs, hardened in alcohol, sections were made and examined according to the most approved methods for proving the existence of bacteria. Grey tubercles were also crushed, spread out on glass covers, dried, and then examined with reference to the existence of micro-organisms. All attempts to find bacteria or other micro-organisms in these prepared specimens proved unsuccessful. In former experiments it had been attempted to color the bacteria as strongly and as differently from the surrounding tissue as possible, and in such attempts it had been proved that in certain cases the addition of alkalies to the color-solutions offered essential advantages; therefore this treatment was adopted. Of the usual analine color the methyline blue will bear the greatest addition of alkali, on which account this coloring material was chosen, and just so much potash-lye was added to a watery solution of the same as to form no precipitate, and that the liquid remained clear. For the preparation of this mixture 1 ccm. of a concentrated alcoholic methyline-blue solution and 200 ccm. of distilled water were mixed, well shaken and during repeated shaking 0.2 ccm. of 10 proc. potash-lye was added. When glass-covered preparations had been treated twenty-four hours with this color solution, there appeared in the tuberculous mass very fine staff-shaped forms, which, as further investigation proved, had the power of increasing and forming spores, and therefore belong to the same group of organisms as the inflammation-of-the-spleen bacilli. In section preparations it was incomparably more difficult to recognize these bacilli among the thickly heaped grains and masses of detritus, and it was therefore attempted, following the example of Weigert, who, succeeding in the coloring of the inflammation-of-the-spleen bacilli a different color from the surrounding tissues, to make the tuberculous bacilli more plainly visible, by similar differentiating color reaction. This end was reached by the use of a concentrated watery solution of vesuvian, with which the blue colored, covered glass preparations and section preparations were treated so long, till to the naked eye, it seemed colored brown. Under microscopic examination it was then seen that only the previously blue-colored cell grains and the products of their disorganization had taken the brown color, but that the tuberculous bacilli remained a beautiful blue color, and, in consequence of this were very plainly to be distinguished from their surroundings, so that even in the masses of grains, thickly heaped together, they were easily recognized. In the use of methyline blue in the manner just described, the bacilli, however, do not take a very intense color, and it requires a certain amount of practice to be able to prove their existence everywhere in tuberculous objects.

Another method which gives to the bacilli a very strong color, we owe to Ehrlich. I use the same now exclusively, and earnestly recommend it to all who are beginning their studies of tuberculous bacilli. Ehrlich's method has since received many unimportant modifications, partly improvements. Among the latter I would reckon the proportions of solutions as settled by Weigert and the shortening of the color solution, a change recommended by Rindfleisch. If I describe the method in which I use Ehrlich's treatment as exactly as possible, I am nevertheless not of the opinion that the modification which I have followed is the best, or that just as good results are not to be gained by other modifications of the treatment. But the coloring of the tuberculous bacilli appears still to offer difficulties to many investigators, and for this reason, it will certainly not seem superfluous to give as exact directions as possible for the method of coloring.

In order to prepare the color solution, aniline water and saturated alcoholic solutions of methyl violet (to be distinguished from methyline blue) or fuchsine are necessary. The aniline water is prepared in the following manner: About 5 ccm. of pure aniline, an oil-like liquid, at first colorless, afterwards becoming brown, is poured into 100 ccm. of distilled water and this mixture is shaken repeatedly. From three to four per cent. of aniline dissolves in the water and the rest remains in the bottom of the dish in the form of thick drops. After a saturated solution of aniline in water has been formed in this way, which is the case after about half an hour, this aniline water is filtrated through a filter, which has been moistened in order to separate it from the rest of the undissolved aniline. The filtrate must be clear as water and colorless, and no little drops of aniline must be suspended in it. If such have passed the filter, the liquid must be filtrated again.

One obtains the second ingredience of the color solution, the saturated solution of methyl violet, by taking not too small a quantity (20 grm.) of dry methyl violet in a well closing glass vessel, pouring over it 100–150 ccm. of absolute alcohol and shaking it repeatedly. After standing a day, there must still be undissolved methyl violet at the bottom of the vessel, which of course can also be dissolved and made use of by gradually pouring on more alcohol. When in place of methyl violet, fuchsine is used, which seems to offer certain advantages for permanent preparations, one also proceeds in the just described manner.

After this, the alcoholic methyl violet solution and the aniline water are to be mixed, and according to Weigert in the proportion of 100 ccm. aniline water to 11 ccm. methyl violet solution. I add to this mixture 10 ccm. of absolute alcohol, because I have found that then the color solution remains usable in a well closed glass for about ten days and does not need to be filtered each time before using.

The preparations which are to be examined with reference to tuberculous bacilli are to be prepared in the following manner: Covering glasses are to be freed from fat and all other extraneous matter, which might prevent adhesion of the substance to be examined, by washing in nitric acid and cleaning with alcohol. The substance is then to be spread out on the covering glass in as thin a section as possible. This procedure succeeds best when soft caseous masses are treated; they can be spread out evenly and thin with a scalpel or a needle. Firmer, crumby caseous masses must be carefully crushed with the scalpel and arranged on the glass by spreading out repeatedly. Still more difficult is it to prepare a little tuberculous knot, which possesses a compact consistence. It must be completely crushed and pressed to pieces on the covering glass. The preparation of covering glasses with sputum also demands a special technique. One must not content himself with taking any chance list of mucus from the sputum, since the sputum consists not only of the secretion of the diseased parts of the lungs, but also of bronchial secretion and mucus from the mouth and nose. It is on this account necessary to examine only those parts of the sputum which have separated themselves from the diseased lungs, that is to say, the yellowish lumps which often swim solitarily in the frothy slimy liquid, which to be sure often forms the greatest part of the sputum. Such a lump of this yellowish, extremely tough mass should be drawn to the edge of the glass, then a little bit of it separated with the scalpel, drawn out of the liquid and on to the inner wall of the glass. Here it can easily be further divided, and be taken off in as large particles as one wishes to transfer to the covering glass. On this it is spread out very evenly and thinly, and any residue should be brought to a corner of the covering glass, and from there removed with blotting paper.

After the covering glass has been prepared in this manner, the section spread out upon it must be allowed to become thoroughly dry. Not until this is the case can the covering glass be heated temporarily, in order to make the section insoluble in watery fluids, with which it is now brought in contact. The covering glass can be put into a drying box heated to 110° for twenty minutes, or one can hold the covering glass with a pincette, and draw it several times, not too quickly, through a gas or spirit flame. The prepared section of the covering glass is during this process to be on the upper side and is not directly touched by the flame. That the forms of the bacteria cells, etc , which occur in the section are not changed in the least by this careful process, can be shown by the following ex-

periment. Of several covering glasses, provided with a dried on section, let the
first not be heated at all, the second drawn once through the flame, the third
twice, etc. When after this the covering glasses are treated with color solutions,
it appears that the coloring of the cell grains and bacteria shows no difference
between the one not heated at all and those drawn through the flame from one
to four times. Also the forms remain unchanged. If the heating is carried farther and the covering glasses oftener drawn through the flame, the bacteria
gradually lose the power of taking the coloring material, while the cell grains
become colored even after very intense heating. In the covering glasses which
have not been heated the section separates itself more or less, often entirely, also
the dissolving "eiweisskörper" (white-of-egg bodies) form with the coloring
matter precipitates, which cover the section and make the recognition of bacteria
very difficult and even impossible. Better results are given by the covering
glasses which have been once or twice drawn through the flame, but those drawn
through three times give the best. One of these last the section clings uniformly,
the "eiweisskörper" are insoluble or so nearly so that no more precipitates are
formed, also the bacteria and cell grains take the color, with an even degree of
intensity, while the surrounding substance remains wholly or almost wholly uncolored. On this account I always proceed thus: After the sections spread out
on the covering glasses have become completely dry, which always takes place in
a few minutes, I draw them three times with moderate quickness through a Bunsen
burner. The color-solution is placed in a watch glass or a flat vessel, and after the
heating the covering glass is laid face downward on the liquid, that it swims.
One must be careful that there are no air bubbles under the glass, as otherwise
the section would not be wet in these places and therefore not colored. Then
let the color-solution be so far heated that it just begins to bubble, and after
once boiling leave the coloring glass upon it about ten minutes; the result will be
a sufficiently powerful coloring. Better results are nevertheless reached when
the covering glass swims for several hours on the unheated solution. In all difficult cases, when one wishes to prove the existence of single bacilli, it is well to
leave the covering glass twelve hours or longer in the color-solution.

When one wishes to examine sections of tissues with reference to tuberculous
bacilli, pieces of the organ in question, not too large, are to be well hardened in
absolute alcohol. Other hardening processes make difficult or even hinder the
coloring of the bacilli. The sections need not be very thin, because by means of
the double coloring, single bacilli can be distinguished very easily even in quite
thick sections. Nevertheless, it is more to the purpose to prepare large sections,
since the distribution of the bacilli is often very irregular, therefore it is possible
that in small sections no bacilli may be found. The use of the microtome in the
preparation of the sections is for this reason almost invaluable. The sections are
immediately laid into the color-solution and remain in the same at least twelve
hours. They can remain in it several days without injury.

The sections as well as the layer clinging to the covering glass have, when
taken out of the color-solution after the given time, a dark blue, almost black-blue
color. In this condition all parts of the tissue are almost evenly dark colored,
and it is scarcely possible to recognize the coarser structures. In order to make
the preparation suitable for microscopic investigation, a great part of the coloring

material must be removed again. This can be done in various ways. In the method originally used by me, of coloring with alkaline methylene-blue solution, I had found that the blue coloring of the constituent parts of the tissue could be driven out by treating with a solution of vesuvian. The same can be carried out in the preparations which are colored according to Ehrlich's method. When these preparations are rinsed off in water and then put into a concentrated watery solution of vesuvian, moved back and forth in the same, and finally put into alcohol, one succeeds in almost completely drawing out the dark blue coloring. The preparations, nevertheless, lose their color more quickly and completely by Ehrlich's method of treating them with nitric acid. That this can be done by other aniline coloring materials, as for example the above mentioned vesuvian, I have mentioned only for the reason that by many the effect of nitric acid has been erroneously held for something specific, but this is not the case, since other acids work similarly.

For taking the color out of the preparations, nitric acid, which has been diluted with two parts of water, is commonly used. So strong a concentration of the acid is nevertheless not absolutely necessary, and of late I use acid diluted with from three to four parts of water. Perhaps one can go even farther in the dilution. One should take care, however, that the nitric acid is free from nitrous acid.

When I spoke of the uncoloring of preparations by means of nitric acid, I followed the description which Ehrlich gave of his process. By the treatment of the covering-glass preparations with nitric acid, this term is exact, when the preparations are not intensely colored; after a stronger coloring, which gives decidedly better and more reliable results, the nitric acid after a few minutes fails to take all color from the dyed section, and section preparations, which, as it has already been carefully shown, must be colored a longer time and very intensely, always keep, after the nitric acid treatment, quite a dark coloring. The expression "uncolor" is not to be understood literally. The failure of bacilli-coloring appears in most cases to have had its foundation in this very thing. The experimenters thought that the preparations after treatment with nitric acid must be wholly colorless, and in order to reach this, partly colored too little the preparations, and partly left them too long in the acid.

When section preparations have lain in the solution twelve hours, and are then put into nitric acid, they lose their black-blue color in a few seconds and take a greenish-blue appearance. If they are then put into distilled water, the tone of the color changes directly. It becomes again noticeably darker and changes into blue, with a bit of violet. The nitric acid, therefore, has left a coloring matter in the preparation, which is insoluble in water, and in connection with water takes a darker tone. That this remainder of coloring matter is not easily soluble, even in nitric acid, can be easily shown. If the section be again dipped into the acid, their color will again become greenish-blue, but not paler than in the first treatment with the acid, and if washed again with water, they will again take the former dark coloring. I conclude from this that a longer remaining of the preparations in the acid is of no value for their further uncoloring, and leave them therefore, only a few seconds, at the highest half a minute in the same. On the contrary, I have found that the coloring matter in the preparations remain-

ing unaffected by nitric acid, is soluble in alcohol from sixty to seventy per cent.
if the preparations are put immediately from the acid into the alcohol. A longer
remaining of the preparations in alcohol appears to make the coloring matter
finally insoluble also for alcohol, and it is therefore to the purpose not to wash
the preparations in water after their treatment with nitric acid, but to place them
directly into the alcohol.

The method of uncoloring followed by me is as follows : By the help of a
platinum wire, which is melted into a little glass staff, the preparations are lifted
out of the color-solution and laid into nitric acid diluted with three to four parts
of water. In this they are moved back and forth for some seconds, until they
have taken a greenish blue color, and are then put directly into a vessel with 60
per cent. alcohol. In the alcohol they remain only about ten to fifteen minutes,
after which they receive the after-coloring now to be described.

In preparations treated with nitric acid and alcohol the component parts of
the tissue are wholly colorless, or possess only a slight bluish tone of color, while
the tuberculous bacilli have retained an intense blue color. Relative positions of the bacilli to their surroundings, are, owing to the nature of the preparations, difficult of proof. It is also very difficult to find single bacilli in the
tissue, whose structure is made as good as completely invisible by the peculiar
method of illumination, which will be described later, and for this cause it is
necessary to give to the tissues a coloring of the nucleus. In order to obtain as
striking a contrast as possible, between the coloring of the bacilli and the cell-
grains, a yellow or light brown is chosen for the supplementary coloring material,
when the bacilli are blue ; a green or blue is chosen when they are red. For the
first case vesuvian is best adapted, for the second methyline blue. Both coloring
materials must nevertheless be used only in weak solutions, and not for too long
a time, in order that just sufficient coloring of the grains may be obtained, lest
single bacilli be hidden by too darkly dyed masses of grains. I use for the second coloring a watery, freshly filtered vesuvian-solution, which to a depth of 2
ccm. is just barely transparent. On this the uncolored covering-glass preparations
are so laid that they float with the prepared section downwards. Section preparations remain in it some minutes. It is not necessary that the section preparations, when they are brought from the alcohol into the vesuvian solution, should
be completely colorless, because they must later be again treated with alcohol, in
order to get rid of the water in them, and will then lose whatever blue coloring
matter will have remained.

One takes the preparations out of the vesuvian solution and puts them again
into ten per cent alcohol and out of this into absolute alcohol. The further treatment is the familiar one, only it is to be recommended that for brightening the
preparation, instead of oil of cloves, oil of turpentine, or still better, cedar-oil be
used, as these do not draw the aniline out of the preparations. With reference
to enclosing them with Canada balsam, I would say that a balsam diluted with
oil of turpentine appears to be the best adapted. Very thick balsam, which must
be warmed in order to enclose the preparation, must not be used, because in
warming, the tuberculous bacilli usually lose their color quickly.

Covering glass preparations can be examined immediately after the washing
off of the vesuvian solution with water, or they can be dried again and enclosed

in Canada balsam. For the examination of the sputum with reference to tuberculous bacilli, the second coloring can as a rule be omitted, so that the microscopic examination of such sputum preparation follows immediately upon the treatment of the same with nitric acid and alcohol.

For the sake of a general view, I will recapitulate briefly the whole coloring process: covering glass preparations dried in the thinnest possible section, after the drying, three times heated in the flame; section preparations of objects, which are well hardened in alcohol; coloring of a solution consisting of 100 ccm. of aniline water, 11 ccm. of alcoholic methyl violet solution or fuchsine, 10 ccm. of absolute alcohol; the preparations remain in the color solution at least twelve hours (the coloring of the covering glasses can be shortened by warming of the solution); treatment of the preparations with diluted (1:3) nitric acid for some seconds; washing in 60 per cent. alcohol for several minutes; (for covering glasses, moving back and forth in alcohol several times is sufficient); second coloring in diluted vesuvian solution or methyline blue for several minutes; washing again in 60 per cent. alcohol, getting rid of water by means of absolute alcohol, brightening in cedar oil; microscopic examination of the preparation; enclosing of the preparation in Canada balsam if the same is to be preserved.

As to the microscopic examination of the objects prepared in this manner, all that I have said in other works[*] about objects colored for the microscope, holds true also for these. In this case also structural relations, which make themselves manifest by the varying refractive power of the single parts of the tissue, are not to be settled; it concerns us only to see the various color relations of the microscopic objects, that is to say, representations of absorption, as clearly and sharply as possible. The structural image whose effect is only disturbing must therefore be gotten rid of, which, as I have shown, can be done most completely with the help of the well-known illuminating apparatus of Abbe. The peculiar illumination which this apparatus affords when it is used without "abblendung," cannot be borne by all systems of lenses. The last must be constructed with special reference to this method of illumination. The greater an opening angle a system possesses, the better it is adapted for the observation of the images of absorption, with help of Abbe's illuminating apparatus. For this reason oil-immersion systems can accomplish the most in the investigation of colored objects.

The covering-glass preparations, if rightly prepared, must possess so little thickness that the structure is formed of a single layer of objects, and in and of itself is little to be considered. These preparations can on this account be examined simply in water and in case of need, a system of water-immersion is sufficient for them, if the field of vision be sufficiently brightened by a condenser. In the case of section-preparations, it is, on the contrary, impossible to set aside the structure formed by so many layers of tissue one above the other, unless the preparation is laid in a liquid which has high power of refraction. It is necessary to do away with the differences in refraction of the tissue, and to use the full illuminating power of Abbe's apparatus, and must use its full power to the best advantage through the large opening angle of an oil-system. One may easily con-

*Untersuchungen ueber die Aetiologie der Wundinfectionskrankheiten. Leipzig 1878, p. 31, etc.

Mittheilunengen aus dem Kaiserlichen Gesundheitsamte. 1881, Vol. 1, p. 9.

vince himself of the necessity of the optic helps here described as absolutely necessary, if one first examines a properly colored section in water and examines it microscopically by a dry system or a water-immersion system and a comparatively narrow "blendi" (blind or opening). Fine distinctions of color, and small colored bacteria in tissues, which are to any extent rich in grains, can under these conditions scarcely be distinguished. Also placing the section in glycerine changes almost nothing, because the differences in refraction of the parts of the tissue are equalized much too slowly and insufficiently. A noticeable improvement is gained by brightening the preparation by means of highly refractive liquids, such as oil of cloves, oil of cedar, etc.; for the brightening rests upon the more or less thorough destruction of the structure-image. But even this improvement is not sufficient to allow the color-pictures to appear in full clearness and sharpness. Only the quantity of light pouring in from all sides by means of Abbe's illuminating apparatus and the oil-system can fulfill this task. Who only cares to examine covering-glass preparations, without caring for complete certainty with regard to the state of things, for him a microscope with water-immersion system and without illuminating apparatus, will in case of need prove itself sufficient. Dry systems are not to be used for bacteria investigations. As soon as reliable investigations of finer bacteria are to be undertaken, or if one wishes to gain an independent judgment as to the newer results of bacteria research, it is absolutely necessary to have at hand the very best optic helps, that is to say oil-immersion systems and Abbe's illuminating apparatus. With regard to the magnifying powers which must be used for the examination of tuberculous bacilli, I will remark that 500-700 fold magnifying power is most to the purpose, and that this is best reached with an oil system $\frac{1}{12}$ of an inch and the corresponding oculars.

In the practical use of the coloring processes just described, the component parts of the tissue of the body conduct themselves almost without exception differently from the tuberculous bacilli. While the latter, in spite of the treatment with nitric acid, alcohol and vesuvian, keeps the dark blue color which they have taken, the remaining animal tissues, as already mentioned, lose the blue color again, and in the second coloring the grains of the cells as well as the products of destruction of the latter, further the little grains of the plasma-cells are dyed brown. Only some parts of the tissue make an exception, as hair and epidermis, which remain more or less blue-colored. Since in these last tuberculous bacilli are hardly to be sought for, the finding of bacilli in the tissues is made exceedingly easy, by their characteristic conduct towards aniline coloring matters. Even in the closest masses of grains and in the midst of broken down cells, which often take all possible forms, from the smallest little points and micrococci-like forms, to the longish staff-like forms, one can with absolute certainty distinguish single tuberculous bacilli from these closely similar forms by means of their dark blue color, which in the brown-colored surrounding and owing to the light-absorbing power of the brown ground appear as staffs almost colored black. This noticeable difference in the color-reaction holds nevertheless, as must constantly be repeated, only for the method of coloring described here. A different preparation of the objects than the quick and good alcohol hardening of the organs, made the condition here, appears to bring about other relations. For while usually the little grains of the plasma-cells conduct themselves like the cell-grains and show a different coloring from the tuberculous bacilli, I have lately seen a preparation, made by Dr. Benda's assistant in the pathological institute in Göttingen, in which tuberculous bacilli were not to be found, but on the contrary the grains of the plasma-cells showed themselves colored blue. Probably in this case the object from which the section was prepared had received a treatment with cromic acid or had not been hardened quickly enough in alcohol.

Accident comes to our help in proving the existence of tuberculous bacilli, since not alone the parts of the tissue take a different coloring, but also all other bacteria which I have known until now and examined, with the exception of the lepra-bacilli to be mentioned later, also react in an opposite manner from the tuberculous bacilli under Ehrlich's method of coloring. Bacteria coming from the mouth are almost always to be found in phtisic sputum. I have never seen that one of these numerous sorts of bacteria showed the same color-reaction as the tuberculous bacilli. This observation has been confirmed by many reliable investigations, and can be considered as an established fact. The same is true of the tuberculous bacilli occurring in the contents of the intestines, when tuberculous ulcers are present. When this sort of discharge is prepared and colored in the prescribed manner on the covering glass, it appears to consist almost wholly of bacteria; they fill the layer in such thick masses. But without exception they take a different color from the tuberculous bacilli, and especially is this the case in the smaller sorts of bacilli, which might perhaps lead one to mistake them for. A peculiar behavior is shown by a large sort of bacilli, which form somewhat large, oval spores standing on ends, in that the spores often keep a plainly manifest, sometimes indeed an intense blue color, while the substance of the bacillus is itself dyed brown. According to all appearance these spores only take the color a short time after their formation, but remain uncolored after they are older. Among the many spores of the contents of the intestines which belong to other sorts of bacilli, until now none have been found which took the color of the tuberculous bacilli. Also the spores of the inflammation-of-the-spleen bacilli, hay bacilli and others, which Dr. Gaffke examined at my instance with reference to this color-reaction, remained uncolored. On the contrary Dr. Gaffke found during these investigations that the spores of "shimmel-pilze" take a strong blue. Also a certain kind of yeast seems to take the color. Since a mistaking of tuberculous bacilli for the above mentioned spores and yeast is impossible, their diagnosis so far as it rests upon the color-reaction is not thereby prejudiced.

Of late I have examined many sorts of bacteria-bearing substances, such as decaying meat infusion, decomposing urine, blood milk, vegetable infusion, mire from swamps with Ehrlich's coloring method, but have never found bacteria which take the same color-reaction as the tuberculous bacilli. I must therefore consider all claims for the appearance of bacteria which conduct themselves in regard to color exactly like the tuberculous bacilli, and which are said to be found in sputum, decaying liquids, the contents of the intestines in healthy men and in swamp-mud, for mistakes and resting upon an erroneous use of the coloring method. I feel myself so much the more justified in this opinion since I almost daily see examples of the difficulties which the use of this certainly rather complicated color technique offers to most people.

Aside from the tuberculous bacilli, until now only one sort of bacteria has been known which takes color in the same way as the tuberculous bacilli; these are, as I have already mentioned in my first communication, the lepra-bacilli. This fact is so much the more worthy of notice, since not only the parasites belonging to tuberculosis and to lepra are similar in many ways and plainly nearly related, but, as is well known, those two diseases stand very near to each other anatomically as well as ætiologically. To be sure, the coloring properties of the two sorts of bacilli are not identical. For although the lepra-bacilli can be colored by the same process as the tuberculous bacilli, the opposite is not the case. The first take, as is well known and as Neisser first proved, the nucleus-coloring of Weigert, which the last do not. However similar the two bacilli are in figure, size, &c., as soon as it comes to a diagnostic distinction, it becomes easy to recognize them through their different response to Weigert's nucleus coloring.

The example of the lepra-bacilli already teaches that the tuberculous bacilli occupy in no way an entirely exceptional position in regard to their response to coloring matters; it is therefore not improbable that in course of time other sorts of bacteria will be found, which possess the same or similar coloring properties as the tuberculous bacilli. But any influence on the apprehension of the ætiological importance of the tuberculous bacilli would not be exercised by such a discovery. For the special reaction against coloring matters is nevertheless not the only specific property of the tuberculous bacilli. They possess, as we shall see later also in biological relations, a number of other peculiarities, which give still more weighty reasons for separating them from the known bacteria as a specific sort.

In all such considerations it is very much to the point to bring to remembrance how the same relations exist in inflammation of the spleen. One will then see that inflammation-of-the-spleen bacilli possess no specific coloring qualities and nevertheless, as is universally acknowledged, are bacteria of a distinct kind and form the cause of inflammation of the spleen. Exactly the same might be the case with tuberculous bacilli if they did not accidentally distinguish themselves from other bacteria by color-reaction. If the latter is nevertheless a fact, it is certainly of value in diagnosis, but it is a great error to think that with the specific color-reaction of the tuberculous bacilli, their ætiological importance stands and falls.

Further it appears to me not improbable that in the near future still further methods may be found by means of which tuberculous bacilli can be colored. Ehrlich's coloring method has already experienced many modifications, of which theoretically the most worthy of notice is the fact found by Ziehl, that aniline can be replaced by other substances, such as phenol,—$C_6H_4(OH)_2$—resorcine, &c. The statements of some authors, that the tuberculous bacilli may be dyed with pure fuchsine appear to hint that still other ways exist in which the coloring can succeed. The diagnostic importance of Ehrlich's method, even if other methods which have no exclusive character are found, suffers by no means. For that remains in spite of all a well established fact, that by strict following of Ehrlich's method the tuberculous bacilli conduct themselves in a manner wholly peculiar to them and are thereby to be distinguished from all till now known bacteria. The method has the value of a chemic reaction, which has made possible the distinction of substances difficult to divide, nevertheless only under the condition that it be used exactly according to the given directions. It would be of special interest to be able to give the bacilli a brown or yellow coloring, because only under this condition would it be possible to get usable photographs of the tuberculous bacilli. Of late I have, to be sure, succeeded, with the help of a previously given treatment of the preparations, with a very weak solution of kali ($\frac{1}{10}$ p. M.) to color the tuberculous bacilli a quite intense brown, nevertheless the preparations do not meet the demands required for photography. It is to be hoped that this difficulty will be overcome. But for the present I have been obliged to do without photographs, however much I have wished by means of photographs to render possible a reliable comparison between the form and size of tuberculous bacilli and other similar ones.

As another hindrance in the coloring of the tuberculous bacilli the temporary character of the coloring must be mentioned. After a shorter or longer time in the preparations enclosed with Canada balsam, the color of the bacilli begins to lose its intensity, very gradually it becomes less noticeable and finally vanishes completely. The preparations colored with methyl-violet and gentian violet pale most quickly, for in some cases the color of such bacilli vanished in two days. The preparations colored with fuchsine keep much longer, as do those colored with alkaline methyline blue solution. Why it is that the color is so fleeting, while the same color in the dyeing of other bacteria have proved themselves unchangeable for years, I am not able to say. But from the circumstance, that in a great number of prepared specimens single ones have been found which have preserved the color completely unchanged for almost a year, I must conclude, that some sort of conditions are present and may be found, which will make possible the retaining of the color.

Moreover the preparations which are so pale have not become entirely useless, as with little trouble they can be colored again. The Canada balsam must be liquified by heat, the specimen taken off carefully with a pinsel and put into oil of turpentine. After 24 hours it is laid in absolute alcohol and after another 24 hours into the color solution to go through the whole coloring process again. The tuberculous bacilli take the blue color just as intensely as at first, but their surroundings, on the contrary, appear less beautifully and clearly colored than before.

A reliable explanation of the difference between tuberculous bacilli and other bacteria in their action in regard to coloring matters appears to me impossible for the present, on account of the insufficient knowledge of the more delicate structure of the chemical constitution. On many grounds it seems likely that the tuberculous bacilli are surrounded by a coating, which acts differently toward coloring matter than the contents, as we already know to be the case with other bacilli. The bacilli dyed with methyline blue appeared thinner than those dyed with methyl violet or fuchsine. One sees in the groups in which the bacilli lie closely pressed together, that the methyl violet colored bacilli move, and the bacilli dyed with methyline blue and appear thin, are separated from each other by plainly manifest spaces. Further, the coloring of the bacilli intensely dyed with methyl violet in growing pale does not vanish uniformly, but an outer layer grows pale first, so that of the thick bacillus a thinner still intensely thread remains, which possesses about the thickness of the bacillus colored with methyline blue. Finally the firm cleaving together of the bacilli in the groups also speaks for the presence of an enwrapping substance which joins them. It is therefore thinkable, that a coating exists, possessed with special properties, and enwrapping the bacilli, and that this allows the entrance of coloring matters under the simultaneous influence of alkali aniline and similar matters, but is on the contrary more or less impenetrable for acids. But in the face of the facts now known, one cannot go farther than to conjectures.

If I now go over to the description of the tuberculous bacilli themselves, although they were first made visible by the help of coloring matters, it appears nevertheless to the point, first to describe their properties as they make themselves known in a living condition and without being influenced by any sort of reagents. To get preparations for this sort of observation, only such tuberculous substances can be used as contain considerable masses of bacilli, because single bacilli cannot be distinguished with certainty in the masses of detritus without help of the color reaction. For this purpose I have used little tuberculous knots from the lungs of guinea pigs, after I had convinced myself by coloring of the great quantity of tuberculous bacilli in them; the little knots were crushed in a drop of blood serum free from bacteria, the substance spread about as finely as possible in the liquid, a drop of this liquid sufficiently large for microscopic examination spread out flat on the under side of a covering-glass and fastened with vasiline on to a hollow object-holder, in order to avoid disturbing currents in the liquid and a too quick evaporation. In a preparation prepared in this manner, in the microscopic examination conducted in the usual manner, that is to say in a suitable "abblendung" of the light by diaphragms, there are found among opaque heaps of indeterminable nuclei, brighter spots in which the formed elements lie less thickly, and here one notices numerous colorless, very fine and short little staffs. The same are mostly united in small groups; in those which lie singly aside from the so-called molecular motion, no motion of their own is to be noticed. The length of the little staffs is about from one-quarter to one-half of the diameter of a red blood corpuscle. An organization is not be noticed in them, and one cannot reorganize their relations to the surrounding cells in this sort of examination, and if no farther observations could be made, one would rather believe he had some sort of lifeless forms before him than bacteria.

If such a covering-glass be lifted up from the concave object-holder, so that the bacilli-bearing substance be dried and then doubly dyed in the manner already described, then the numerous grains and remains of cells appear dyed brown, the little staffs on the contrary receive an intense blue coloring and distinguish themselves sharply from all known component parts of the animal tissue with which they are mixed. The bacilli do not show themselves in their full number until after their coloring; they may be distinguished not only on the thinnest spots of the preparation, but everywhere with full certainty, even among the thick heaps of cells. It is noticeable that the little staffs appear thinner after the coloring than in the uncolored condition, the reason for which is, that before the coloring they must be observed by light cut off by diaphragms, in which case the lines of interference on the borders of the object appear to enlarge its diameter, while the observation of the colored bacilli is made in full light falling upon it from all sides, through which all phenomena of interference are excluded.

In like manner one can examine the most various objects by spreading out the substance to be examined as to its contents of tuberculous bacilli on the covering-glass and by coloring the same. Nevertheless, one does not learn much more than that the bacilli are present in a tissue or in a liquid and in what quantity they are present. Their position and their relations to the surrounding tissues cannot, in this way at least, be determined. The examination on the covering-glass is therefore sufficient for liquids, but for tissues can only have a preliminary, provisional character. Only the examination of the prepared sections of hardened parts can give reliable information as to the presence and diffusion of bacilli in the tuberculously altered organs.

To find out whether bacilli are regular accompaniments of tuberculosis, I have examined as extensive a ground as possible. Materials for this investigation I have received for the most part from Dr. Friedlaender, who, at my request, and in the most obliging manner, made the rich material of the city hospital in Friedrichsham accessible to me, and from the director of the city hospital in Moabit, Dr. Guttman, who committed to my charge a number of cases of tuberculosis for examination. It is a pleasant duty in this place to thank both gentlemen for the help they have given to my work.

In the following description of the results gained in these investigations I must, in order to make a general survey, omit the historical enumeration of the single cases in the order in which accident placed them in my hand, and will speak of them as grouped according to the usual anatomic points of view. Before I turn to this, however, I must make a few general remarks. When a little tuberculous knot is examined in prepared sections, without the use of nucleus-coloring, and without the diffused light of Abbe's illuminating apparatus, it appears like a body formed of cellular elements thickly crowded together and therefore only slightly transparent. As soon as the little tuberculous knot becomes caseous in the centre the cells change into a more or less fine grained, almost opaque mass, in which fine details are not to be distinguished. But a thoroughly different image of the tubercle is gained when the prepared sections are laid into strongly refractive media and the examination is undertaken after the nucleus-coloring, and by diffused illumination. The youngest tuberculous knots then show themselves to consist of colored grains heaped together. Nevertheless the grains are not so closely packed but that a section of ordinary thickness appears transparent enough to make it possible to distinguish the most delicate form elements occurring in the space between the grains. The caseous centres of the tuberculous knots in the prepared section appear wholly changed; they appear almost uncolored and completely transparent because there the cells have died and take no coloring; only here and there in them are found the remains of nuclei going to pieces, in the form of colored grain groups which, to be sure, are pretty closely pressed together but still allow all single form elements to be distinguished. Larger caseous herds conduct themselves in the same manner. The caseous substance itself has become completely transparent by the treatment and shows only a light greyish-yellow color tone interrupted by single brown grains or groups of grains. Every single tuberculous bacillus can be distinguished with ease. The conceptions of the microscopic image of the tubercle and of the tuberculously altered tissue which usually obtain are to be modified according to the circumstances just described when the examination of the pictorial reproduction of prepared specimens with nucleus-coloring and illuminated by diffused light is concerned.

As to the qualities of tuberculous bacilli in general, as they manifest themselves in the colored condition, the following is still to be mentioned.

They always appear in the form of little staves whose length, as has already been given in the description of uncolored bacilli, is equal to $\frac{1}{4}$—$\frac{1}{2}$ of the diameter of a red blood corpuscle (about 0,0015—0,0035 mm). The diameter of the thickness is as constant as the length of the bacilli is variable, provided that one and the same coloring method is used. Under the coloring method first used by me, with alkaline methyline blue solution, they appear considerably thinner than with the use of Ehrlich's method. It is difficult to fix the slight size relations about which we are here concerned without the use of photography. When I look through a considerable number of my bacteria photographs for bacilli which correspond best as to size with tuberculous bacilli, I find in F. Cohn's " Beitrage zur Biologie der Pflanzen ," II Vol., 3 Book, in the photographs given in Plate 15, No 1, among club-shaped bacilli with spores fixed in their ends, very thin and small bacilli which, if magnified 700 instead of 500 times as in the photograph, would come nearest to the tuberculous bacilli. There are among these bacilli also some which are spore-bearing and which about give a representation of the spore-bearing bacilli to be mentioned later. Also in the bacilli taken from blood putrefaction in mice (Mäuse septicämie) and shown in this work, Vol. I, Plate VII, Fig. 41, are bacilli almost as thick, but on the average somewhat shorter than tuberculous bacilli.

The tuberculous are usually not completely straight little staves ; one usually finds slight breaks or bends and sometimes a crookedness which in the longest specimens goes so far as to suggest screwshaped windings. By this varying from the straight-lined forms the tuberculous bacilli distinguish themselves from other bacteria which come noticeably near them in size relations according to the photographs.

The distribution of the bacilli in the tuberculously-altered tissue is a very varying one. Sometimes they are heaped together in dense masses, so that by a very slight magnifying power bacilli-bearing spots can be recognized by their blue color. Very frequently, however, they are present only in small numbers. One finds the bacilli with most certainty where the tuberculous process is just beginning or is in a state of rapid growth. Here they are to be found in moderate numbers and between the nuclei of the cells which are heaped together and which usually show the epithelioid character at an early stage. After a more careful observation it is manifest that a bacillus almost always lies close beside a nucleus, and that it is to be found in the interior of the cell belonging to this nucleus. One cell can often contain two or even three bacilli. In places where the disease has made greater progress the number of bacilli usually increases extraordinarily. They then often group themselves into little heaps closely pressed together, in which the bacilli lie parallel and are connected, so closely that it is often difficult to recognize the fact that the group is composed of single bacilli. In this arrangement the tuberculous bacilli bear a great resemblance to the lepra bacilli, which are mostly grouped in this manner. The relation of the tuberculous bacilli to the cells cannot be decided in this stage, because the cells have already experienced great changes and are in process of dying. Their nuclei begin to decompose and to change themselves into irregularly formed grains of very varying size. Gradually these become scarcer and there remains a uniform mass which will not take nucleus coloring and in which all the cells originally present have died. This mass forms what was formerly considered the essential part of the tubercle, as the bearer of the infectious material, namely, the caseous centre of the same. But, as a rule, this caseous substance is very poor in tuberculous bacilli. Only when the death of the cells and their change into the nucleusless caseous mass has taken place very quickly are the bacilli visible for a time in considerable numbers. It is plain that they retain the capacity of fixing the coloring matter longer than the cells perishing under their influence. But very soon the bacilli themselves undergo farther changes, either dying or go into the stage of spore formation, in which they gradually lose their power of taking color. In the last case only their spores remain in the caseous substance, and as until now no means have been found of coloring the spores of tuberculi in any way whatever, their presence after the vanishing of the tuberculi betrays itself only by the infectious qualities of the caseous substance in which they are imbedded. On account of the importance, formerly and even very lately, erroneously attached to the caseous products of the tuberculous process, it may not be superfluous emphatically to direct attention to the facts that in all tuberculous affections the tuberculi appear first, collections of cells joining themselves to these; and that the dying of these cells and the caseous change resulting from this are secondary processes.[*]

The opinion which still, to a great extent, holds ground that the relation between the bacilli and the caseous degeneration is the opposite of this, that the becoming caseous represent the primary, and that by means of this a suitable breeding ground is prepared for the tuberculous bacilli, is therefore completely erroneous. For the anatomical comprehension of the tissue changes in consequence of tuberculosis the process of becoming caseous may be of interest, but for the ætiology of tuberculosis it has not the slightest importance.

If I have lately been charged with paying too little attention to the process of caseous degeneration in my account of the ætiology of tuberculosis, the charge is unfounded, for it rests upon a misunderstanding of my standpoint, since I have only treated the ætiological relations of tuberculosis, but have left the pathological details to the pathological anatomists, especially when they lie so far aside from ætiology as the caseous changes of the tuberculous tissue.

Of greater importance for the questions interesting us here are the relations of tuberculous bacilli to the gigantic cells so frequently appearing in tuberculously altered tissues.

These peculiar formations are so frequent in tuberculous tissues that it was for a time believed that they must be considered as characteristic of tuberculosis. Since the gigantic cells are almost always situated at the centre of the little tuberculous knot, the opinion has often been expressed that the tuberculous virus must be contained in their interior —has indeed been pointed out in the shape of very small grains.

---

[*] Baumgarten, "Ueber die Wege der tuberkülosen Infection." Zeitschrift f. klin. Med. Bd. VI, heft. I.

It has now been shown to be certain that the gigantic cells occur in other
disease processes and are not specific products of tuberculosis. Nevertheless the
conviction that the infectious material must be contained in the gigantic cells has
proved itself correct. For as soon as gigantic cells appear in the tubercles, tuberculous bacilli are almost regularly found in them, and the relation of bacilli to
gigantic cells is a manifold one.

In all slowly developing tuberculous processes, for example scrofula, spongy
inflammation of the joints, etc., in which the bacilli are present only in scanty
numbers, we find the bacilli almost exclusively in gigantic cells, and then always
only one or at most a few specimens in each cell. But when, corresponding with
the more or less intensive course of the process, the bacilli appear in considerable
numbers, then the gigantic cells which may be present are more generously supplied with them, and the number of bacilli enclosed by a gigantic cell may reach
fifty or more.

A single bacillus in the interior of a gigantic cell is sometimes not easily recognized, for it often happens that the little staff may not be in the horizontal
plane of the prepared section, but is placed diagonally or perpendicularly, and
then appears in the microscopic image not as a blue line but only as a point,
which can only be traced to a certain distance and its staff form recognized by
raising and lowering the tube. Since the contents of the giant cell take a
more or less brown-color tone, the little staff does not always show itself in the
characteristic blue, but in a darker, almost black color, the reason being that aniline brown absorbs the blue part of the spectrum, and therefore a blue object
observed through a brown solution, must appear black. Attention should, by
this opportunity, be given to the fact that bacilli never look blue but always black
when the ground on which they are seen is brown, when, for example brown-
colored nuclei lie under them.

Although, as already said, it may sometimes be difficult to find a single bacillus in a gigantic cell, bacilli which in considerable masses fill a giant cell give a
so much the more striking picture, which cannot be overlooked, even by a weak
magnifying power. In this case the giant cells appear like little blue circles
which are surrounded by a brown wall, the nuclei of the giant cell.

The arrangement of the bacilli in the giant cells often takes a very peculiar
form. When the nuclei of the giant cell form a closed ring, and, for example,
only one bacillus is found within it, the same generally lies in the centre or at
least only a little excentric.

The nuclei of the giant cell are often forced toward one end, that is in a uni-
polaric arrangement, especially if the cell possesses an oval figure, or one even
longer in proportion to its width. In this case the bacillus is usually found in the
part of the cell free from nuclei; it often takes a position exactly opposite to
them, and lies in the extreme point of the nucleus free pole. In the observation
of the giant cells the supposition involuntarily forces itself upon one that a sort
of antagonism exists between the nuclei of the giant cell and the parasite enclosed
by it, which effects the greatest possible distance between the nuclei and the
bacilli. This remarkable opposition between nuclei and bacilli is most noticeable
in those giant cells whose nuclei are grouped equatorially and which then a
bacillus in each of the nucleus, free poles, or by a bipolar arrangement of the

nuclei in which, each heap of nuclei holds a bacillus as it were in check.

Also where larger numbers of bacilli are observed in giant cells the oppositional grouping of nuclei and bacilli can be noticed. Usually, however, an entirely different arrangement of bacilli occurs. It looks as if with increasing numbers the behavior of the bacilli towards the nuclei became more active. They force themselves, namely, more and more towards the periphery of the cell, squeeze themselves between the nuclei and finally break through the wall of the nuclei.

During this process it is very worthy of notice that the bacilli, in this case, regularly place themselves with their axis perpendicular to the surface of the giant cell, so that in a microscopic image if the upper curvature or the base of the gigantic cell be shown, they appear as points; when, on the contrary, the greatest diameter of the cell is show, we get the image of a circle of rays formed of blue staffs.

Such a great increase in the number of bacilli appears regularly to be followed by the destruction of the giant cell; for in the neighborhood of giant cells supplied with radiately arranged bacilli, especially towards the interior of the tuberculous herds, one often finds groups of bacilli which show the radiate arrangement, but are no longer enclosed by brown-colored nuclei. Moreover, since many transitional forms are found, it cannot be doubted that such radiated groups of bacilli mark places in which giant cells were formerly found whose nuclei have vanished, and of whose contents only the bacilli remain.

By the help of the microscopic images just described one can read about the following conception of the relations of bacilli to the cell contents of the tubercle without losing oneself in too venturesome hypotheses. The first stage in the development of the tubercle is the appearance of one or more bacilli in the interior of cells which bear an epithelioid character. How the bacilli get there can scarcely be explained, otherwise than that they are taken up from already existing tuberculous herds and carried along by such tissue elements as possess motion of their own, that is to say, by wandering cells, be they in the blood, the lymph, or in the tissue itself, for the bacilli possess no motion of their own. Only so is the peculiar fact to be explained that frequently single bacilli or little groups of the same are found dispersed at quite uniform and comparatively great distances from each other, as, for example, in scrophulosis, fungous and lupous tissues and in general in all chronic tuberculous affections. For a wandering cell which has taken up a bacillus takes therewith no such harmless burden as if it swallowed a grain of cinnabar, a particle of coal or other indifferent material. Laden with the latter it can still go over much ground, but under the deleterious influence of the bacillus changes occur in the wandering cell which soon bring it to a standstill. Whether the wandering cell perishes, and the bacilli are taken up by other cells present at the spot, which last then take an epithelioidal character; or, as appears to me more probable after my investigations, the wandering cell transporting the bacillus itself changes into an epithelioid cell and after that into a giant cell must be decided by studies directed to that special point.

For the assumption that the bacilli are originally carried along by wandering cells, and that their dispersion in the tissue depends upon this, the following reasons can be given: In the first place I would like to bring to remembrance an analogous process in which also staff-shaped bacteria are incorporated by the colorless cells of the blood. This case is the putrefaction of the blood in mice (Mäuse-septicämie) described by me in the "Investigations of the Ætiology of Infectious Diseases." In this disease bacilli very similar to the tuberculous bacilli are to be found in the interior of the white blood corpuscles, and at first there are only one or two specimens close to the nucleus; then they increase very rapidly in the cell, destroying the nucleus and finally bursting the cell in order, having become free, to be again taken up by other cells and to prepare for them a rapid ruin, so that in a short time the majority of the white blood corpuscles are found inhabited by bacilli. The tuberculous bacilli grow, as we shall see later, very much more slowly than the bacilli of septicämie (putre. of blood), and the cells laden with them can therefore manifest vital functions very much longer. The further course of both diseases is, in accordance with this fact, very different, in spite of the fact that the first beginnings of the bacteria invasion possess such great similarity.

Direct observation also speaks in favor of the assumption that tuberculous bacilli are first seized and transported by the wandering cells. This can best be recognized in the cases in which considerable numbers of bacilli are introduced directly into the course of the blood, for example, by injection into the ear veins of the rabbit. If an animal infected in this manner be soon killed, one still finds in the blood numerous white blood corpuscles which enclose one or more tuberculous bacilli, and moreover in the tissue itself of the lung, liver and spleen, genuine round cells appear which are provided with a simple or divided nucleus, still possess no epithelioid form, therefore exactly resemble the colorless blood cells and yet contain tuberculous bacilli. Another explanation of this, other than that they are wandering cells which took up the bacilli in the course of the blood and transported them into the neighboring tissue, will scarcely be found Also in the case of guinea pigs into whose bauchhöhle (belly cavity) considerable numbers of tuberculous bacilli were injected, and which died in the course of the first week, the same appearances were found.

A third ground for this assumption appears to me to lie in the fact that in dead tissues, in such places, therefore, wherein the influence of the living cells upon the bacilli is completely excluded, when a lively growth of the bacilli takes place, they arrange themselves in typically formed groups which resemble the peculiar forms of the bacteria colonies in reinculturen of the same on blood serum. We must therefore consider these forms to be those taken by tuberculous bacilli when developing undisturbed and when their grouping is decided only by the variations and changes of place conditioned by their growth. Every other arrangement is to be looked upon as the working of some sort of disturbance, for example, that caused by currents in the liquids, or by the direct influence of movable tissue elements. So the relative positions of the bacilli in the giant cells, especially their position as opposed to the nucleus, and the radiating arrangement appear to me to be conditioned upon currents in the plasma of the cell, and not by motion belonging to the bacilli themselves, since the bacilli after the death of the cells do not change the radiating arrangement once taken. After the wandering cell which transported the bacillus has changed itself into an epithelioid cell and given up moving from place to place, the pathogenic influence of the bacilli prepares to spread itself out upon the neighboring cells existing within a certain circuit. Whether they have proceeded from cells already present in this place in consequence of the attraction exercised by the bacillus itself, or rather by the materials produced by it and diffused into the surroundings, all cells situated within a definite region change into epithelioid cells. The cell containing the bacillus suffers still greater changes. It grows constantly larger, while at the same time the nuclei constantly increase, and it finally attains the shape and size of the familiar giant cells. That the development of the giant cells really goes on in this manner can be seen from suitably prepared sections, which show all stages of development from simple epithelioid cells with one bacillus to the completely developed giant cell with many nuclei and many bacilli. As most suitable for the study of the development of giant cells I should consider the tuberculous tissue of cattle and horses, which is especially rich in giant cells and in which I have often seen the above mentioned transitional forms. The further fate of the giant cells is a varied one, according as the progress of the disease is rapid or slow. In the last case the number of bacilli enclosed by a giant cell is always a limited one. Usually there are only one or two. It is indeed scarcely to be thought that the bacillus found in a large giant cell is the same which caused the formation of the cell. One finds not infrequently in a giant cell a bacillus which is no longer so intensely colored as other bacilli in neighboring gigantic cells; I have also seen cases in which the giant cell contains a dark and strongly colored bacillus, and beside it a second, very pale one, which without careful attention would be overlooked. Furthermore I have sometimes found spore-bearing bacilli in the interior of giant cells. From all this I conclude that the giant cell is quite a durable formation, that the bacilli, on the contrary, do not possess such duration of life, and that they can only maintain themselves for a considerable time in giant cells, in that a new generation follows a dying one. Sometimes they form spores in the interior of the giant cells, and in this case leave behind them the germs of a later generation. But often enough the vegetation of the bacilli in the cell appears to die out and the empty cell then remains as a monument of their former presence. When one, as is often the case in a tuberculous tissue, finds quite numerous giant cells, and among them only comparatively few supplied with bacilli, one can then take for granted that many of the apparently empty gigantic cells contain spores of tuberculous bacilli; others, on the contrary, mark the places of former vegetations of bacilli, and one is tempted to institute a comparison with a volcanic region in which occur not only single active volcanoes, but a great number slumbering for a time, or completely extinct, these latter nevertheless bearing unmistakable marks of their former activity.

As to the fate of giant cells when the bacilli in them increases rapidly, we have already spoken. In this case the result is exactly opposed to the one just described; the giant cell is the conquered party; it is, as it were, burst by the tuberculous bacilli forcing themselves through the wall of nuclei. Its nuclei perish, dissolve themselves into little grains, and the cell perishes.

How it is that at one time the bacilli are conquered, or for a long time remain confined to definite spots and barely hold their own, that at another time their number increases rapidly and all cell elements in their neighborhood quickly perish, only suppositions can be made, which cannot here be entered upon, but which I will discuss later.

The further changes which complete themselves in tuberculous tissue after the formation of the epithelioid and giant cells are all of a regressive nature. For the greater part they belong in the sphere of the processes described by Weigert as necrosis of coagulation, and lead to the death or the tuberculously diseased tissue and to the formation of the so-called caseous masses which so frequently form the interior of the tuberculous-herds. The tuberculous bacilli usually vanish very quickly in the caseous masses, so that they are only to be met in younger herds, and are almost always wanting in older ones. In other cases after the vanishing of the bacilli vegetation, the tuberculous tissue may simply shrink and be changed into firm cellular tissue.

A very important property of the tuberculous bacilli must be mentioned here. It is the spore-forming property. As is well known, F. Cohn was the first to observe in the so-called hay-bacilli the appearance of shining little bodies which remained when the bacilli perished, had the power of germinating and growing to bacilli, and were to be considered the fruit form of the bacilli, receiving hence from F. Cohn the name of spores.

The appearance of the spore formation as it shows itself microscopically in bacilli tinged with aniline colors, is to be seen in a very instructive manner on photograph No. 76, Plate 13, in the first volume of these communications. The bacilli appear there with short joints, and mostly consisting of two joints. Some of these joints are evenly dark colored and still resemble completely the spore-free bacilli on photograph 75.

In many joints one notices, nevertheless, the appearance of a light point which increases in size gradually, while the colored contents of the joint withdraw more and more to the two ends, and the sides are bordered by fine lines marking the outlines of the joint. The bright space in the interior of the bacillus joint is the spore which in this specimen shows itself not by its brilliancy, since it is imbedded in a strongly light-refracting substance, but only by the absence of coloring material. With few exceptions the bacilli spores do not take the aniline coloring. The division into the articulation does not always appear so sharply defined as in the bacilli of this picture.

In many sorts of bacilli, as for example in those belonging to inflammation-of-the-spleen, the members appear closely joined together and form a continuous thread which contains the uncolored spores at regular intervals. The spore formation of the tuberculous bacilli conducts itself in like fashion. The bacillus preserves its connection and does not fall apart into separate joints, but a bright body appears in every joint so that the bacillus after coloring resembles a little dark thread interrupted by bright egg-shaped spaces. By the use of the strongest systems and great magnifying power it may then be shown that the spore-bearing tuberculous bacillus presents exactly the same appearance as the spore-bearing bacilli of inflammation-of-the-spleen, only in greatly diminished proportions. The spores are egg-shaped, bounded by a delicate colored line, and are present usually in the number of two to six in one bacillus. Since every single spore takes possession of one joint, from their numbers we can decide upon the number of the joints of the bacillus, that is to say of the single elements out of which the same is formed. If a substance containing spore-bearing tuberculous bacilli be examined in the uncolored condition and in less strongly refractive liquids, the bacilli appear to be provided with brilliantly shining little bodies; these last can therefore not be vacuoles or simple gaps in the protoplasm of the bacillus, but must be genuine spores.

After these remarks as to the universal qualities of tuberculous bacilli, I now turn to the description of their action in the various tuberculous processes.

A. TUBERCULOSIS IN MAN.

I.—MILIARY TUBERCULOSIS.

Nineteen cases in all were examined in which the tubercles were found in the form of miliary and sub-miliary little grey knots, mostly provided with a whitish or weak yellowish centre, scattered in several organs, lungs, brain, liver, spleen and kidneys. The bacilli were wanting in the tuberculous knots in no one of these cases. The smaller and younger the knots were, so much the more plentiful were the bacilli, and they were thickest at the centre. As soon as the middle of the little knot will no longer take nucleus coloring, as soon, therefore, as the caseous degeneration begins, the number of bacilli decreases immediately. In the larger knots, whose centres had already experienced a far-reaching caseous change, few bacilli were to be found, and those only to be found between the nuclei of the epithelioid cells occurring in the periphery of the knot. Now and then one finds in the giant cells occurring on the border of the caseous herd, single bacilli or groups of the same. A noticeable feature which re-appears in the chronic processes of the lungs is this, that most giant cells contain black pigment grains beside which the bacilli are still easily to be distinguished. In other organs I have not seen such pigment-bearing giant cells, and their presence appears to be limited to the lungs. From the analogy of other results obtained from the lungs of swine and other animals, to be mentioned later, I might suppose that we here have before us giant cells which originally developed in the interior of an alveolus and took into themselves the pigment of the perishing cells present in the alveolus. This view is taken by Watson Cheyne on the ground of direct observations of giant cells which were found in alveoli of the human lung. (See Practitioner, April, 1883). These cells, which first developed in the alveoli next to the little knots, are afterwards taken up by them as the knots extend. In many of the older knots the bacilli appear to have vanished completely. Nevertheless, we must remember that the prepared sections of the larger tubercles always contain only fragments, and that if the bacilli are wanting their absence from the whole knot is not thereby proved. The relations here are similar to those formerly described in regard to the giant cells, that is to say, that beside those knots which still contain abundant bacilli others occur in which the bacilli have either entirely vanished or have left spores behind them. Nevertheless, if a sufficient number of sections are examined, one almost always finds spots rich in bacilli, and it would not be right from the results of a few specimens to give a judgment as to the presence or absence of bacilli in miliary tubercles.

In miliary tuberculosis of the liver and spleen, I have seen bacilli almost exclusively in the giant cells. Especially in the spleen, beside completely developed tubercles, there are often found giant cells of considerable size, which are almost isolated or only surrounded by a few epithelioid cells, and are regularly the seat of one to three tuberculous bacilli.

The tubercles of the membrane of the brain were, almost without exception, rich in tuberculous bacilli. Frequently the latter are found in the immediate neighborhood of small arteries beside which are spindle-formed heaps of epithelioid cells; between the latter the bacilli are strewn in quite uniform numbers. But in many places the bacilli are present in such thick masses that their presence makes itself known, under a weak magnifying power through the blue color of the parts in question. In this case they are principally round cells, therefore younger cell formations, among which the bacilli vegetation has its seat. Sometimes also I have seen bacilli in the interior of the vasa.

Of miliary tubercles of the choroidee only one case was at my disposal, and that I owe to Prof. Weigert. Here also were formed herds without nuclei, (that is to say already developed caseous degeneration), which were surrounded by large giant cells, and many epithelioid cells. Partly in the giant cells, but also partly outside of them, between the epithelioid cells, a good many tuberculous bacilli were present.

With the exception of one case, comparatively old caseous herds were always to be found, especially in the lungs and bronchial glands. Also in these herds, which may be considerd the point of departure for miliary tuberculosis, the presence of bacilli were proved in the cases which were examined with reference to them. Often, to be sure, they were only found sparsely in the periphery of the herd, but sometimes one discovered nests of dense masses of bacilli.

It would lead too far if I should here describe particularly all the cases of miliary tuberculosis which I have examined, and I select, therefore, only some of the most characteristic.

1.—Workman, thirty-six years old. Strong man, who had not felt unwell until fourteen days before being taken to the hospital, attacked with coughing; pains in the chest and moderate fever. The symptoms observed in the hospital were only slightly characteristic, and corresponded with those of catarrhal pneumonia. Under increase of dyspnœ the patient's powers sank rapidly and he died four days after his reception into the hospital. In the journal of dissection the following is worthy of mention. The pleura on both sides occupied by numerous little miliary knots. Both lungs infiltrated, greyish-red, and many little miliary grey knots present; the larger knots show caseous degeneration. In the conus arteriosus of the heart several sub-miliary grey knots of the endocard. On the closing border of the mitralis eruption of firm knots varying from miliary to the size of a pea. In the liver not very numerous little knots. Both kidneys contain grey little miliary knots in the pithy substance as well as in the outer coating in abundance. The hollow of the right kidney dilated, and in the same two defecti with indented borders and caseous base whose diameter is about 1½ to 2 cm. A caseous deposit of the size of a hazel nut in one papilla. Bladder free from tubercles. In the prostata some caseous deposits. In the urethra abundant little miliary knots. Caseous degeneration of the accessory testicles, partly with caseous softening, drawn in scars on the scrotum. In the testicles themselves abundant deposits of little grey miliary knots. The thoracic duct dilated, on several spots on its wall caseous thickening, and on the inner surface of the same some defecti provided with caseous base.

Here we had a case of chronic tuberculosis of the uro-genital organs. The tuberculosis of the thoracic duct connected itself with this and had as a consequence, the breaking out of the general miliary tuberculosis. This case according to its origin belongs to the form of miliary tuberculosis described by Ponfick and forms a typical example of the same. The microscopic returns corresponded exactly with the description of the action of the bacilli as previously sketched. The tubercles in the lung tissue showed themselves comparatively small, and for the most part contained bacilli in abundance. Some contained so many that under a weak magnifying power a bluish color showed itself in the middle.

Many gigantic cells were also found in the tubercles of the liver and spleen, which for the most part were supplied with bacilli. Very numerous bacilli were present on the edge and in the surroundings of the herd in the papilla of the kidneys. At single points in the surroundings of this herd, the bacilli had collected in groups in the urethra, and the peculiar grouping here manifest suggested the figures which they take in blood serum cultures, and which are to be mentioned later. Whether the bacilli in this case reached the urethra via the course of the blood or whether they spread from the neighboring tissue, could not be decided. In another tuberculous kidney which I received from Prof. Weigert, numerous glomeruli and the neighboring urethra were covered with masses of bacilli, which leads us to conclude that the bacilli can make their way from the course of the blood into the urethra and from there perhaps into the urine.

2.—A second case of tuberculosis of the thoracic duct in a man forty-eight years old shows an analogous behavior. The tuberculous process had been here spread from the caseous mediastinal glands to the thoracic duct, and has brought about miliary tuberculosis of the lungs, liver, spleen and kidneys. Death followed later than in the first case; the tuberculous eruption was not so abundant, the single knots reached a greater size, were more caseous and contained a correspondingly smaller number of bacilli.

3.—Nine year old boy. Said to have been taken sick only a few days before his admission into the hospital. At his entrance into the hospital diseased sensorium, great restlessness and delirium with high fever. In the following days bronchial phenomena showed themselves, death ten days later. Dissection showed: caseous swelling of the bronchial glands; broncho-pneumonia herds in both lower lobes of the lung. Besides these, numerous grey miliary and submiliary tubercles in the lungs, in the enlarged spleen, in the liver and in the kidneys. At the base of the brain, and in the surrounding of the vessels a slight muddiness (trübung) and a great number of little grey knots.

In the tubercles of the lungs, liver and kidneys and spleen, bacilli were found in varying abundance. The tubercles of the pia mater were very abundantly supplied with them.

In the caseous bronchial glands belonging to this case, large quantities of bacilli were found, and not only on the borders of the caseous herd, but forcing themselves far into it. The parts of the gland tissue which were not yet necrotized contained numerous gigantic cells which were noticeable for the multitude of enclosed tuberculous bacilli, and for the radiate arrangement of the same.

Plainly the tuberculous process in the bronchial glands had only lately began and had spread rapidly. The gland tissue had become very quickly necrotized and softened under the influence of the tuberculous bacilli. Somewhere there must have been a breaking through into a vasalumen (gefässlumen) and so considerable numbers of bacilli have got into the course of the blood to have caused the general eruption of miliary tubercles. The location of this breach was, however, not to be found in this case. That the same is not always easy to find may be seen from the following case.

4.—A strong man of about thirty years died after a sickness which showed typhoid symptoms and had not lasted longer than three weeks. From the dissection it appeared that there were very many grey little miliary knots in the lungs, liver and kidneys, as well as in the greatly enlarged spleen. The bronchial glands were swollen, of a marrow-like nature, but not caseous. Also, moreover, no older caseous herd could be proved, in spite of the most thorough investigation, so that one was loth to make a diagnosis of miliary tuberculosis. The intestines and mesenterial glands were not changed.

Microscopic investigation gave the following very noteworthy result: Sections from the bronchial glands showed wide-spread spots bare of nuclei, and which were only filled with black pigment grains, and numerous fragments of perished nuclei, together with dense swarms of tuberculous bacilli. These last were heaped together in such masses in the immediate neighborhood of little arteries that the vasalumen (gefässlumen) appeared to be surrounded by a blue court, even under a slight magnifying power. A greater magnifying power showed these blue masses to be composed of bacilli. In single places the bacilli forced themselves even into the interior of the vasa, and there could be no doubt, therefore, that they found their way into the blood in this manner, and were transported in all directions in great quantity. A third method was thereby sought by which a general tuberculous infection and the miliary tuberculosis conditioned upon it could take place, after Ponfick had succeeded in discovering one of these ways in the thoracic duct, and after Weigert had taught the second, and to all appearance by far the most frequent, in the breaking through of tuberculous masses into the veins.

The miliary tubercles of the spleen and lungs contained a good many bacilli, partly also in the giant cells.

But this case was of great interest in another way. It appeared, namely, that numerous capillaries were filled for short distances with micrococci. Under the double coloring treatment, the tuberculous bacilli took, as they always do, the blue coloring, the micrococci, on the contrary, the brown color. In many places in the same field of vision, and at slight distances from each other, brown colored micrococci and blue colored bacilli were to be seen. The capillary micrococci embolism were moreover very numerous in the lungs, and especially in the spleen. They had not as yet led to striking changes in their surroundings, such as heaping together of nuclei or necrosis, and must therefore have appeared not many days before death. The combination of a bacilli and a micrococci invasion as it occurred here, belongs to the mixed infections whose appearance seems not to be rare. Such mixed infections can be generated artificially in animals by simultaneous or closely following inoculation with various infectious materials, for example, by using inflammation-of-the-spleen and septicæmic bacilli in the case of mice. Also tuberculosis and inflammation-of-the-spleen can exist simultaneously in the same animal. I have inoculated a number of guinea pigs which were tuberculous to a great degree with inflammation-of-the-spleen bacilli. In consequence of this, the animals were attacked with inflammation of the spleen and died. Several of them had very large numbers of tuberculous bacilli in the lungs and spleen, and in sections from these, by double coloring, the tuberculous bacilli took the blue, and the very numerous inflammation-of-the-spleen bacilli took the brown color. As a further instance of a spontaneously arising mixed infection, the occurrence of micrococci herds in typhus is to be noticed. Further, Brieger and Ehrlich[*] have drawn attention to a combination of typhus with malignant œdema, in which case the very fitting expression mixed infection was first used. It is therefore plain that we have such a mixed infection in the case here spoken of. The tuberculous disease of the bronchial glands formed the primary infection, which, in consequence of the rapid growth of the bacilli and their forcing themselves into the arteries, led to general miliary tuberculosis. Not until this disease was well established, the strength of the organism had been very much lowered, and therewith probably the ground for the micrococci invasion had been prepared, did the latter follow; proceeding to all appearance from an ulcerated defekt (imperfection) on the tongue, and causing in connection with the miliary tuberculosis, death so much the more quickly.

A similar combination of tuberculous bacilli in the miliary tubercles of the lungs, and micrococci in the neighboring vessels, has been observed by Watson Cheyne, [†] and it may therefore probably be accepted that with a little attention this sort of mixed infection might be not infrequently found.

Of the other case of miliary tuberculosis coming under examination, the following may be briefly sketched :

5.—Boy of eight years. Caseous bronchial tubes, numerous miliary tubercles in the lungs, spleen, liver and kidneys. The little knots of the lungs were thoroughly provided with large nucleusless caseous centres, and on the circumferential parts of the same, single little groups of bacilli were to be found. Tuberculous bacilli could also be proved in some giant cells on the border of the caseous centers. Bacilli-bearing giant cells were also to be found in the spleen. In this case I did not succeed in finding bacilli in the little knots of the liver and kidneys. On the contrary they were abundantly present in little nests in the bronchial glands.

6.—A strongly built and vigorous man, thirty-four years old, had suffered from a cough for about three weeks before his entrance into the hospital. Quite high fever and broncho-pneumonia symptoms, cerebral phenomena soon appeared, and by means of the opthalmoscope, tuberculosis of the choroidea could be clearly shown. Death followed fourteen days after entrance to the hospital. Caseous confluent herds in the tips of both lungs, quite large, not very thickly sown miliary tubercles in the lungs, spleen and liver, bronchial glands caseous In the little knots of the lungs tuberculous bacilli found singly in the periphery.

---

[*] Berl. klin. Wochenschrift 1882. No. 44.
[†] The Practitioner, Vol. XXX. No. 4, Apr., 1883, p. 295.

Liver and spleen contained giant cells, among them some with bacilli. In the bronchial glands also, small groups of bacilli could be shown only in a few spots.

.7.—Baker's apprentice, seventeen years old, anæmic, of a delicate build, had coughed for half a year, was taken into the hospital with a pleuritic exudation from the right side. Puncturing the thorax brought out 500 ccm. of clear serous liquid. Four weeks later cerebral symptoms appeared, and after another two ' weeks death followed. Dissection showed tuberculous pleurisy, miliary tuberculosis of the lungs and tuberculous meningitis. In the little knots of the lungs, as also in those of the pia mater, tuberculous bacilli were found and in some places very abundantly.

8.—Six-year-old girl. Bronchial glands and partly verkalkt (ossified.) Single lobuläre (lobular, lobe-shaped?) red, hepatized herds in the lungs, within which the bronchiæ were supplied with purulent contents. At the base of the brain muddy "sulzig" infiltrations of the pia. Numerous miliary and sub-miliary knots in the vessels of the fossa Sylvii. Microscopic examination showed tuberculous bacilli in small numbers in scattered spots in the bronchial glands. In the hepatized parts of the lung the alveoli were found filled with bacteria of various sorts. (aspirations pneumonia). The meningeal tubercles were very abundantly supplied with tuberculous bacilli.

9.—Workman thirty-four years of age, drunkard, treated two years before on account of scrofula of the wrist bones. Complication with "lymphangitischen" (pertaining to inflammation of the lymph vessels) abscesses on the upper part of the left foot and upper part of the thigh. Death, with cerebral symptoms, after seven weeks' stay in the hospital. The dissection showed caseous infiltration with formation of cavities in the tips of both lungs, miliary tubercles in both lungs and at the base of the brain. Quite numerous tuberculous bacilli were found in the tubercles of the lungs as well as in the meningeal tubercles.

10.—Five year old boy. Wide-spread caseous degeneration of the bronchial glands. In the tip of the left lung a caseous herd larger than a hazel nut, with the centre in a state of disorganization. A moderate number of comparatively large miliary tubercles in the lungs. Quite numerous grey and yellowish little caseous knots in liver, spleen and kidneys. The pia mater of the basis of the brain greyish, yellow "sulzig" infiltrated. Under microscopic investigation numerous tuberculous bacilli were found, partly enclosed by giant cells, in the bronchial glands; also great heaps of bacilli in the tubercles of the brain membranes. In the little knots of the lungs, liver, spleen and kidneys only comparatively few bacilli were present.

11.—A one-year-old child very much afflicted with atrophy, said to have been taken sick with a cough eight days before its arrival at the hospital. The bronchial symptoms and dyspnœa which showed themselves in the first examination, increased, and the child died two and one-half weeks later. The right upper lobe of the lung was found to be caseously infiltrated, bronchial glands caseous. Numerous miliary tubercles on the peritoneum, on the diaphragm and in the spleen. Tuberculous meningitis. In the meningeal tubercles numerous tuberculous bacilli. Nests of bacilli in the caseous parts of the lungs and in the bronchial glands. Scattered bacilli in the tubercles of the peritoneum and diaphragm, exclusively enclosed in giant cells. A moderate number of bacilli in the tubercles of the spleen.

2.—PHTHISIS OF THE LUNGS.

Twenty-nine cases were examined and the tuberculous bacilli were wanting in none of them. The number of bacilli, to be sure, varied greatly, but one could recognize here as in miliary tuberculosis, in so far a connection between the number of the bacilli and the phthisic process, that the bacilli were found most abundantly in fresh caseous infiltrations and in the interior of cavities whose environment was in a state of rapid decay. The bacilli were found less abundantly in the cavities provided with compact, callous walls; they were most scarce in scarred, shrivelled lung tissues containing much pigment. The more their number decreases the more they confine themselves to the interior of the giant cells. One may not conclude, however, that each single case conducts itself throughout in a like manner in regard to bacilli, that one phthisic lung shows throughout a great number of bacilli, another, on the contrary, only scattered ones. To be sure it may sometimes be so, but it will usually be found that in the same lung some parts are entirely free from bacilli, but that in single spots dense nests of the same are present. So especially may cavities of some extent appear almost or wholly free from bacilli, until, by continued investigation, one suddenly finds one or more nests of tuberculous bacilli in a hidden side indentation or encamped close beside the wall of the cavity, but not yet melted into it, and finds them, too, so thickly crowded together that even under a low magnifying power they appear as dark blue spots. For the examination of phthisic lungs it follows that one may not content himself with looking through a number of sections from any one spot, for example from a piece of the wall of a cavity, but should examine as great a variety of places as possible, and should take not too small a number of specimens from each. Only so can one get a correct conception of the behavior of tuberculous bacilli in the case in question.

After the experience gained in my investigations I should represent the relations of the bacilli to phthisic processes in the following manner : In the beginning only a few, or single bacilli get into the lung, and on account of their slow growth are very soon enclosed by a cell infiltration and thereby hindered from forcing themselves more quickly into the surroundings of the infectious spot. The bacilli, nevertheless, do not perish in the cell infiltration, but cause necrosis and caseous degeneration in the centre of the cell mass just as in miliary tuberculosis. The first beginning of phthisis would, if one could succeed in getting a sight of it, completely resemble a miliary tuberculosis. The little knot gradually takes larger dimensions and becomes constantly more unlike the miliary tubercle. An analogy of this stage might be found, however, in the not rarely occurring cases of large solitary tubercles, which do not always appear solitary but also scattered to a certain extent in various organs. These also I would consider as having proceeded from single miliary tubercles whose number is so small that they do not bring about the immediate death of their bearer, as is the case in general miliary tuberculosis, but which rather gain time for farther growth, and can finally grow to caseous herds of a good size. It is quite certain that the phthisic process takes the same development, that, namely, proceeding from a little miliary knot there grows a constantly spreading caseous herd. In the lungs the relations shape themselves very peculiarly, because the increasing caseous herd does not remain closed, but after a shorter or longer time makes its way into the bronchiæ, empties itself and so is changed into a cavity. The further increase of the cavity goes on in a very irregular manner according as the process of vegetation in the tuberculous bacilli makes a halt in single places for a shorter or longer time, or continues, and according to this indentations or shrivelling are formed in places. Taken in general, the cavity, however large or irregular formed, retains the essential properties of the tuberculous caseous herd ; necrotic masses in the interior, joined to these towards the outside nests of epithelioid cells with gigantic cells sandwiched in, and in the giant cells often tuberculous bacilli. An exception occurs only in so far as the tuberculous bacilli in the cavity appear in comparative abundance also in the interior of necrotic masses, which in the caseous herds remaining permanently closed is not usually the case. Probably this has its foundation in the fact that the masses dead, and to a certain extent used up as a breeding-ground for bacilli, are constantly being emptied, and the parting of the walls of the cavity give constantly a new food material for bacilli.

In this manner the usual chronic form of phthisis would run its course. In this usual course the vegetation of the bacilli is a very slow one and the occurrence of the bacilli very sparse, and essentially confined to the giant cells in the immediate surrounding of the cavities and to the contents of the same. The circumstance is very noteworthy that even in comparatively small tuberculous herds the growth and dispersion of the bacilli is not uniform but discontinuous. In large herds, and especially in larger cavities, this behavior, which has already been touched upon, is always more striking. Widespread spaces of the cavity may be wholly free from bacilli and sometimes the bacilli may be confined to single spots of very slight extent. From this we may conclude that the conditions of life for bacilli in a tuberculous herd are not everywhere equally favorable, and probably also in regard to time may be subject to fluctuations. The bacilli must then vanish from the places which no longer give them suitable breeding-ground. In this case at one time only a temporary freedom from the parasites can take place, when the bacilli from the neighborhood later force themselves in or if spores have been left behind which may develop under more favorable conditions. At another time a lasting freedom of the diseased spot from bacilli can take place when the just mentioned conditions for the reviving of the bacilli vegetation do not occur. Shrivelling, scarring and healing will follow then in such a place. One can think that since these things may take place partially in the periphery of the tuberculous herd, the same might happen in the whole compass of the herd, and so a complete healing take place. Analogous relations are found in other diseases conditioned upon bacteria which also spread themselves out centrifugally from the original spot of infection, but can show in their progress considerable irregularities sometimes cease to grow at one point, sometimes thrive and spread rapidly, as is the case, for example, in erysipelas.

The development of a single tuberculous herd running its course in the lung under the type of chronic phthisis can be complicated in many ways, if the tuberculous bacilli in any manner get out of the reach of the original herd into other places and there give rise to the development of secondary herds. This proceeding can complete itself in various ways. The bacilli can get into the larger blood vessels of the lungs, be strewn over the whole body in greater or lesser numbers by the course of the blood and cause miliary tuberculosis. Then, according to all appearance, the bacilli have the power of spreading themselves also by way of the course of the lymph, of forcing themselves into the bronchial glands and causing secondary tuberculous changes. The bacilli conveyed from the cavities into the air passages find by far the most frequent opportunities of fixing themselves in other places. Oftentimes they nestle themselves in other parts of the air passages and more especially into the larynx. Often if the sputum be swallowed they plant themselves in the intestinal passage.

The usual course of the phthisis must then be most affected when the bacilli-bearing pus from the cavities is on the way to be conveyed outward by the bronchiæ, but by some unfortunate disturbance of the motions of respiration is again aspirated and brought into parts of the lung until then healthy. When only a slight quantity, poor in bacilli, is aspirated, it can only bring about the beginning of a comparatively small number of infectious herds. These will gradually grow and develop into cavities according to the place that the bacilli-bearing masses reach, sometimes in the immediate neighborhood of the mother herd, sometimes some distance from it, even in the other previously healthy lung, and will from small beginnings grow just as slowly as the first tuberculous herd. But as soon as considerable quantities of the bacilli-rich contents of the cavities are breathed in, and wide-spread parts of the lung are overflowed, as it were, with infectious material, as appears not seldom to be the case, then the formation of single tuberculous knots is not the first step, but tuberculous infiltrations arise which show us by the lobed and even lobuled (lobuläre) arrangement that they came from the respiratory passages. The penetration of the tuberculous bacilli en masse has not as a consequence heaps of closed cells and the formation of giant cells, as is the case when individual bacilli appear, but necrosis of the component parts of the cells in the attacked tissue spreads widely and with comparative quickness. In consequence wide-spread caseous degenerations form in many places, also rapid dissolution of the tissue, with development of cavities which bear another character than those formerly described.

While these cavities possess compact, firm walls in which are found giant cells and scattered tuberculous bacilli, the walls of cavities formed in the decomposing and widely caseous lung tissue are permeated by a thick bacilli vegetation. They do not consist of condensed callous tissue, which only melts away slowly under the influence of the bacilli, but the wall allows us still plainly to recognize the structure of the alveoli which are filled with the caseous substance rich in bacilli, but are in the act of losing their coherence, and falling to pieces. These conditions are usually described as caseous pneumonia, acute phthisis, etc.

The most various combinations of these two just described processes, that of a tuberculous herd proceeding from a single infectious herd and spreading slowly, and the caseous infiltrations arising from a flood of infectious material, unite to give a most varied conception of the tuberculous destruction of the lungs covered by the general name phthisis.

It deserves still to be mentioned that the aspirated masses giving rise to caseous infiltration do not necessarily always spring from a tuberculous herd of the lung. Several recorded observations of animals are at my disposal which prove that a caseous ulceration of the tonsils, or a tuberculous ulcer on the superior margin of the lower jaw, which had developed itself in a rabbit in consequence of a bite, also in one case a caseous bronchial gland communicating with the air passages, can furnish the bacilli-bearing masses which are breathed into the lungs. On this account therefore, also in man, tuberculous processes in the larynx, throat and mouth, as well as caseous bronchial glands, so soon as the latter empty their contents into the bronchiæ, are to be kept in sight as points of departure for caseous infiltrations of the lungs.

The conduct of the secretion of tuberculous lungs, the phthisic sputum, deserves special consideration. Since tuberculous bacilli occur in no other diseased conditions than in the tuberculous, the demonstration of their presence has great diagnostic importance. The first examinations which I made of phthisic sputum led to the result that abundant numbers of bacilli showed themselves in the sputum in half the cases examined ; in other cases only a few bacilli were to be found, and in many they seemed to be wanting. But when I used Ehrlich's color treatment, and had had more practice among the by no means few cases examined, not one case more occurred in which the bacilli were wanting. I do not mean to say by this, that in single cases, after repeated investigation one may not fail to find bacilli, but in general it must be considered a settled fact, on account of the numerous results in the mean time published also by other investigators, that the bacilli, with few exceptions, constantly occur in phthisic sputum, are wanting in the sputum of other lung diseases, and thereby give an unmistakable diagnostic characteristic mark of the presence of tuberculous affections of the lungs.

The bacilli often occur in the sputum in quite considerable numbers. Apparently these are always cases in which there is rapid dissolving of the caseously infiltrated parts of the lungs, and in which the cavity walls have mixed their secretion with the sputum. The well known caseous fragments which from the beginning have been considered as a specially characteristic component part of phthisic sputum, consist almost wholly of masses of bacilli. One can think that these caseous fragments have arisen from compact bacilli masses, such as are sometimes found on the inner wall of the cavities, becoming loosened, and swept away by the secretion of the cavity. Nevertheless, one often meets cases in which the sputum is very poor in bacilli, and must look through a number of specimens, indeed sometimes must repeat the investigations for several successive days before he succeeds in discovering bacilli. The sputum investigations carried on for a long time by Gaffky with a number of phthisic patients, which are published in this volume of the " Mittheilungen " give the best idea of the frequency of bacilli in phthisic sputum.

Very often the bacilli occurring in the sputum are spore-bearing, and this appears to be especially the case when the bacilli could develop themselves unhindered and abundantly, as is the case in caseous infiltrations. Just these relations are of the greatest importance for the ætiology of tuberculosis, and we shall come back to them later.

Since the sputum is always more or less mixed with saliva, it contains regularly, beside the tuberculous bacilli, other sorts of bacteria, the abundance and variety of these depending upon the amount of saliva and mucus from the cavity of the mouth mixed with it.

If sputum is kept for some time in a vessel the tuberculous bacilli remain unchanged, both in reference to their number and to their responsiveness to coloring matter. The other bacteria, on the contrary, increase rapidly in numbers, other bacteria coming from the air or accidental defilement, appear, and a real decay develops itself very soon. Under microscopic investigation one finds, then, numberless bacteria occurring in the fresh sputum out of the cavity of the mouth, or those appearing in decaying sputum, which act in regard to color like the tuberculous bacilli. The latter always keep their intense blue color if the coloring is carried on according to the rule, while all other bacteria appear dyed brown.

It is still to be mentioned that sometimes bacteria force themselves also into the cavities, and can increase in their secretions so that, in these cases, one finds in the contents of the cavity not only tuberculous bacilli, but other bacteria. I concerned myself, nevertheless, in the few cases over which my observations of this sort extended, only with certain sorts of bacteria, so one need not suppose that a sort of decay in the contents of the cavity, as in the sputum exposed to the air, existed, but it must be assumed that of the various sorts of bacteria which accident had brought into the cavities, only certain definite kinds can thrive there. These then either lead a harmless parasitic life in the contents of the cavity, as for example, the bacteria of the green pus, which I have repeatedly found in large old cavities, or they, as it seems, take part in the destructive work of the tuberculous bacilli, as seems to me to be the case with a special sort of micrococci. The latter distinguish themselves by a peculiar arrangement, almost regularly forming groups of four, and have on that account at first sight a certain resemblance to sarcine, nevertheless in other ways distinguishing themselves essentially from these. Gaffke has studied the properties of these further[*] and found that they are disease-producing for many species of animals. Also, in the case in which they were first discovered, they appear to have aided in the quick destruction of the lung tissue. It is much to be wished that in future attention should be paid to these combinations of phthisis, because they must lead to the finding of such sorts of bacteria as of themselves possess no or only conditional disease-producing properties for the human organism, but under conditions specially favorable to them, as for example in an ulcerous herd of the lung, can form little nests and have a decisive influence on the further course of the process. Of how much importance such secondarily-working bacteria may be has already been mentioned in the description of miliary tuberculosis and the mixed infection occurring there.

In connection with phthisis of the lungs, some remarks may here find place in regard to the phthisis of the intestines. Among the twenty-nine cases which I had the opportunity to examine, I received in addition to parts of the phthisic

---

[*]Langenbeck's Archiv., Vol. 28, Book 3.

lung also, in eight cases pieces of the intestinum tenue with tuberculous ulcerations, and just as often caseous mesentric glands. Several times the abscesses of the intestinum tenue were surrounded by fresh tuberculous erruptions, which followed the lymph-passages.

The growth of the bacilli appears, at least so far as we can come to a conclusion from the material at my disposal, to find more favorable conditions in the intestines than is usually the case in the lungs. It should not therefore surprise us if, in the excrement of a person suffering from phthisic and tuberculous abscesses, tuberculous bacilli occur in comparatively large numbers, as Lichtheim first discovered. Among the numberless and very largely staff-formed bacteria of the intestinal contents the microscopic proof of tuberculous bacilli would have proved itself as good as impossible, if it had not been for the specific tinctorial properties of the latter, which just in this case proved themselves especially useful. Since from several sides the certainty of the proof of tuberculous bacilli in intestinal excrement has been doubted, I urged Dr. Gaffky to undertake a number of investigations. These showed that neither in the excrement of healthy persons nor in those of sick ones, who were not suffering from tuberculous diseases, any sort of bacteria were found which gave the same sort of color-reaction as the tuberculous bacilli. Also in the case of all persons afflicted with phthisis, who were examined in regard to it and who had tuberculous bacilli in the sputum, it was impossible to prove such in the excrement, but they could regularly be shown in such patients when they had plain symptoms of ulcerous disease of the intestines. One observation made by Gaffky during these investigations deserves special mention. Namely, in the contents of the intestines there not seldom occur large spore-bearing bacilli, whose bodies, like those of all other bacteria, take the brown color, while the spores remain colored more or less intensely blue. The spores appear to be more darkly blue the younger they are. When the body of the bacillus perishes and the spore alone remains, since in size it resembles a large micrococcus, it can easily be mistaken for one at first sight; especially when several spores lie near together they can be very similar to a little heap of large micrococci. Probably, therefore, the formations described by Lichtheim as blue-colored micrococci are identical with these spores. But it appears that other bacilli occurring in the intestines form spores, which by Ehrlich's color-treatment keep the blue color, for Gaffky found in the excrement of a tuberculous monkey, beside tuberculous bacilli, bacilli of still larger dimensions than those just mentioned. These had not egg-shaped, but very long-extended, almost staff-shaped, spores. The spores were fixed in the ends, and in bacilli of more than one member so arranged that in two neighboring members the spore-bearing ends were turned towards each other and followed in the manner indicated here: ⸻ ·__· ⸻ ·__· The points are spores, the lines bacilli-members, a peculiar arrangement of the spores to which I on another occasion have already drawn attention.* The spores of the anthrax-bacilli, hay and potato bacilli were also tried by Ehrlich's color-method and did not show the reaction, but it is nevertheless very probable that still other sorts of bacilli-spores act

---

*F. Cohn's Beiträge zur Biology der Pflanzen. Vol. 2, Book 3.

tinctorially as the sorts described, and that with the help of aniline reaction one would be able to distinguish these sorts of bacilli easily from others. The animal in which the bacilli with staff-shaped spores were found, died and had, as the dissection showed, beside numerous tubercles in the lungs, spleen, etc., several tuberculous abscesses in the intestinum tenue abundantly supplied with tuberculous bacilli.

From the cases of phthisis examined I will speak of a few which served as points of departure for inoculation and for the culture of tuberculous bacilli.

1.—A woman of thirty years, whose mother also died of phthisis, suffered for half a year from cough with expectoration. Great loss of flesh. Occasionally slight fever. Death after three months' stay in the hospital. Dissection showed left lung partially deformed as well the upper as the under lobe containing a number of communicating vomicæ. Right lung also deformed, containing a large baylike vomica in the upper lobe and several smaller ones in the middle lobe. Spleen, liver, kidneys free from tuberculous changes. Under microscopic investigation only a moderate number of bacilli were found in the contents of the vomicæ. In the surroundings of the vomicæ, which had compact walls, were giant cells grouped around little nucleousless herds and largely supplied with tuberculous bacilli.

2.—Man twenty-three years of age. His mother said to have suffered from phthisis. Had been in the hospital the year before on account of pleurisy. In the last few months repeated hæmoptisis. Besides this diarrhœa. At his reception into the hospital thin, anæmic. Suffocation and bronchial breathing over the point of the right lung. Cough with purulent expectoration. Death after four months. In the right lung large vomicæ with partly callous, partly caseously infiltrated walls. On the vocal chords tuberculous ulcerations. Beginning amyloid degeneration of the spleen. Numerous abscesses in the intestines, swelling and caseous degeneration of the mesentric glands. Also in this case the tuberculous bacilli were present in comparatively small numbers in the contents of the vomicæ and in the lung tissue, but, on the contrary, were very numerous at the base of the intestinal abscesses and in the caseous mesentric glands.

3.—Workman of forty-three years, quite strongly built. No heredity could be proved. Had suffered for three months from cough, expectoration and increasing weakness. Of late his troubles, especially dyspnœa, had grown much worse. Death after twelve days' stay in the hospital. In the tips of both lungs vomicæ of moderate size, wide-spread caseous infiltration with occasional softening and formation of vomicæ in the middle and lower parts of the lung. Ulceration in the larynx. In the vomicæ as well as in the caseously infiltrated lung tissue, bacilli were found in great quantities.

4.—Man of thirty-two years, not hereditarily burdened. Said to have been sick only four weeks. At his reception into the hospital anæmic, emaciated. Death after six weeks' stay in the hospital. In both lungs numerous vomicæ of varying size whose surroundings for a considerable distance were caseously infiltrated. Some smaller vomicæ lay near the surface and showed as slight protuberances. These were used to obtain rein culturen.

5.—Servant girl of nineteen years; mother died of phthisis; had suffered for a year from cough; of a delicate build, short breathed and had profuse sweats. Death after seven weeks' stay in the hospital In the left upper lobe of the lung a moderately large vomica. The remaining part of the lobe infiltrated and lobular, (lobulärc?) caseous herds, close together, partly with central decay. On the right almost the whole lung infiltrated with greyish yellow caseous masses and with many softened spots. In the trachea flat ulcerations. In the ileum and in the beginning of the colon numerous abscesses with indented borders. Mesentric glands partly freshly caseously infiltrated. As well in the interior of the vomicæ as in the caseously infiltrated parts of both lungs extraordinary numbers of bacilli were found, mostly heaped together in nests. Also in the intestinal abscesses and mesentric gland tuberculous bacilli were present in considerable numbers.

3.—TUBERCULOSIS OF VARIOUS ORGANS.

The cases of tuberculosis examined by me to be mentioned under this division concern single organs which have been obtained, partly from operations, partly from sections, without my knowing anything further of the course of the disease or of the other results obtained from the sections. I can on this account only mention them summarily here.

Two cases of tuberculous abscess of the tongue. At the base of the abscesses and in places forcing themselves deep into the tissue of the tongue, thick swarms of tuberculous bacilli were found.

Tuberculous bacilli were just as abundantly present in four cases of tuberculosis of the pelvis of the kidneys, in one case of tuberculosis of the bladder and of the urethra, once in tuberculosis of the surenal gland, and in a case of tuberculosis of the uterus and of the tubi.

On the contrary, the number of tuberculous bacilli was very small in five tuberculous testicles removed by operations. They could only be proved here singly in the numerously present giant cells.

Just the same behavior showed itself also in two cases of large solitary tuberculous herds of the brain. The appearance of the bacilli here also confined itself to the giant cells.

The only case belonging here in which no tuberculous bacilli at all could be proved concerned the examination of pus which came from a tuberculous abscess of the kidneys. Inoculation with this pus had given a positive result, therefore infectious germs must have been present in the same. We shall speak of this case later and give explanation for the negative result of the microscopic examination.

4.—SCROFULOUS GLANDS.

The scrofulous glands which I have examined I owe for the most part to Privy Councillor Badeleben, who placed the same at my disposal directly after they were removed. Twenty-one cases in all were examined in which the glands showed themselves tuberculous. I understand by this the presence of epithelioid cells which are grouped in herds and enclose more or less numerous giant cells. With few exceptions, in which a necrosis and caseous degeneration of the diseased gland tissue had not yet appeared, these cells were joined directly to the caseous herd present, and formed the immediate surrounding of the same. Only in glands which possessed a tuberculous structure of this sort could tuberculous bacilli be proved. In a number of cases, on the contrary, in which the glands were enlarged, partly also softened, and thoroughly impregnated with herds of pus, but in which epithelioid and giant cells as well as the characteristic necrosis of the tissue were wanting, no bacilli were found.

The tuberculous or scrofulous glands examined belonged to twenty-one different patients. Of these eleven were between the ages of ten and twenty years, seven between the ages of twenty and thirty, one each thirty-seven, thirty-nine, and three. The glands had been situated fifteen times on the neck and in the submaxillary region, three times in the back of the neck, twice in the axilla, and once in the region of the cubitus. In the last case, that of a three-year-old boy, there existed at the same time caries of the wrist on the same side. In three cases there had been a relapse after the first operation, and this had caused a second excision of the glands. In several cases it was stated that phthisis was hereditary in each family.

In general the tuberculous glands in reference to their contents of tuberculous bacilli were very uniform. In the interior of the caseous herd I have found the bacilli only in two cases, and even here only individual specimens. The bacilli appeared only exceptionally and individually between the epithelioid cells. On the contrary, among the giant cells there were always some, occasionally many, which contained one or two tuberculous bacilli. Giant cells with a larger number of bacilli, as one so often finds them in bronchial and mesentric glands, I have never been able to find in scrofulous glands.

In the three cases in which after a time a second gland extirpation took place, the glands twice showed themselves to have the same constitution as in the first examination. The third of these cases, which is noteworthy in other respects, was as follows: strongly built man of thirty-four years. A year before large gland tumors had grown on the neck and in both axillæ, and at the same time a high degree of anæmia had developed. In the lungs no tubercles could be shown. The tumors which had been excised had the figure and size of potatoes, were of a soft, almost marrow-like constitution, and without caseous changes in the interior. The microscopic investigation showed that in the swelled mass numberless little herds of epithelioid cells were imbedded, which contained in their midst one or more giant cells. In many of these giant cells one or at most two tuberculous bacilli were found. Very rarely it occurred that one bacillus was situated in the interior of an epithelioid cell, close beside the nucleus of the same. Scarcely a year after the removal of these glands, almost equally large tumors have developed themselves anew on the same spots. These were extirpated again and showed the same microscopic conduct, only with the exception that the number of bacilli-bearing giant cells had decidedly increased in comparison with the previous tumors.

5—TUBERCULOSIS OF THE JOINTS AND BONES.

There were examined by me thirteen tuberculous joints, three hip joints, five knee joints, three elbow joints, one foot joint, and one finger joint; further, ten tuberculous affections of the bone, thus divided : three times on wrist bones, five times on ankle bones, twice vortex caries (of these last in one case only the pus was examined).   To a great extent I owe this material for examination to Privy Councillor Bardeleben.

The granulation-tissue which is formed in the surroundings of tuberculous joints and bones offers no essential difference in the single cases.   The same appearances repeat themselves constantly in the structure of the tissue and in the arrangement of the bacilli, and resemble completely the description given of scrofulous glands.   One finds just the same more or less scattered and often confluent herds of epithelioid cells which surround giant cells, and also here the occurrence of bacilli is confined almost exclusively to the giant cells.   In the caseous, nucleusless spots, as well as in the pus secretions, the attempts to find scattered bacilli only succeeded in some cases.   Also in this respect tuberculosis of the bones and joints conducts itself exactly like that of the scrofulous glands.

The bacilli could be proved in all the cases. Only in the abscess pus coming from the vortex caries was it impossible to find tuberculous bacilli.   But inoculation with this pus, as was formerly mentioned of the pus of a tuberculous abscess of the kidneys, gave a positive result.

6.—LUPUS.

According to the anatomical investigations of Friedlænder and the positive results of inoculation which Hüter and Schüller have obtained, it was to be expected that lupus must also belong to the group of genuine tuberculous diseases.   I therefore used the opportunity offered to me by Director Hahn, Prof. Küster and Prof. Lewin, soon after the publication of my first communication concerning the ætiology of tuberculosis, to examine a number of cases of lupus in order to gain certainty in regard to this supposition.

Seven cases of lupus were investigated, which all had the most decided symptoms and were watched for a long time in the hospital, so that no doubt of the correctness of the diagnosis can be entertained. From four cases I received excised pieces of the skin, from the other three cases lupus substance scraped out.   For direct microscopic examination only the excised pieces of skin were suitable.   In all four cases, though only a few specimens in each, tuberculous were found, only, however, in the interior of giant cells.   The tuberculous bacilli are so scattered in the lupus tissue that in two cases the bacilli were not found until from one twenty-seven sections, from the other forty-three sections had been examined.   Nevertheless, it happened repeatedly that when in a succession of sections not a single bacillus showed itself, sections followed each other quickly with from 1—3 bacilli.   More than one bacillus I have never seen in a giant cell in lupus.

It may for the present be remarked here that of all the seven cases, inoculations were made into the anterior eye-chambers of rabbits, which without exception produced tuberculosis of the iris, and in those animals which were allowed to live for a longer time, general tuberculosis.   In these tubercles resulting from inoculation numerous tuberculous bacilli were found.   From one case (excised piece of skin from the cheek of a ten-year-old boy suffering from lupus hypertrophicus) success was obtained in getting reniculturen of bacilli, which have also been used for the successful inoculation of animals.

B.—TUBERCULOSIS IN ANIMALS.

By the study of the appearances under which tuberculosis runs its course, in the various sorts of animals, the noteworthy fact is manifest that tuberculosis conducts itself differently in the case of almost every species. However striking this fact at first appears, it nevertheless corresponds to the observations made in regard to other bacteria diseases. So inflammation of the spleen in a similar manner is different in different animals; septicämie of mice, conditioned upon very small bacilli, offers another example, for when it is inoculated it kills mice, but in rabbits only causes an erysipelas-like disease confined to the skin.

Until now no warm-blooded animal is known which is entirely unresponsive to the infection of the tuberculous virus, and one may therefore expect that many varieties will show themselves in the anatomical aspect of tuberculosis in the various species of animals.

However various the forms which the symptoms of tuberculosis may take in single species, and however little one may be inclined to explain human phthisis and a tuberculosis of a guinea pig caused by inoculation as the same sort of disease, nevertheless between these extremes there are found, partly in the same species, still more in other species, transitional forms of tuberculosis which cause the apparent gulf to vanish. But the complete unity of the tuberculous processes of different species of animals shows itself to be irrefutable when we look away from the constitution of the tuberculous organs as seen by the naked eye, and from the secondary changes in the same, such as caseous degeneration and calcination, and keep to the primary structure of the tubercle, which, as we have already seen, repeats itself with typical regularity in all the various processes in man, and equally so in the apparently so different forms of tuberculosis in the various species of animals. The differences in the tuberculosis of different species of animals which most attract the eye concern only those secondary changes which in the one case lead to wide-spread coagulation-necrosis without caseous degeneration (liver and spleen of guinea pigs); in another to rapid softening and the formation of a thinly liquid, pus-like secretion (tubercle of the monkey); further to transformation into hop-like caseous substance (tuberculosis of man); to simultaneous calcination and caseous degeneration (pearl distemper of cattle); to the formation of hard swollen masses with deposited lime "concrementen" (tuberculosis of the fowl)—and so forth. The primary changes in all these cases are histologically exactly alike. Somewhat the same is true in regard to the formation of pus in various animals. So the pus formed in consequence of a simple inflammation in the rabbit and the fowl has an entirely different constitution than that of man, and yet in this case one would not speak of different sorts of pus formation.

It would lead too far if the special peculiarities of every single kind of animal should be described in detail, and I shall therefore be obliged to confine myself to a brief characterizing of the different forms.

I.—PERLSUCHT OF CATTLE.

The tuberculosis of cattle runs its course, as is well known, almost always by the forming of little knots which do not really become caseous and perish, but become calcareous and heap themselves together in such masses that they can finally form great tumors. But beside these there occur widespread firmly caseous infiltrations of the lung tissue, as well as hollow spaces in the lungs, filled with pap-like caseous masses.

Of the last mentioned form only four cases were examined. The caseous contents of the cavities were of such a consistence that when the cavities were cut the contents could be pressed out in sausage-shaped masses. The cavities themselves appeared to have proceeded from enlarged bronchiæ. In their walls were found quite numerous giant cells, and in a number of these last one to several tuberculous bacilli. The caseous masses were, as the inoculations performed with them showed, infectious, yet no bacilli could be found in them. On the places where the "bronchi-ectatischen" cavities approached the surface of the lungs, the usual knot-shaped tumors of the "perlsucht" were found on the pleura, and showed the immediate connection with this form of cattle tuberculosis.

Of this last form eleven cases were examined in which the development of the knots of the "perlsucht" did not confine themselves to the lungs, but reached out to the diaphragm, peritoneum and omentum. Several times the mesenterial glands were tuberculously changed and impregnated with firm caseous herds. The tuberculous bacilli were wanting in no case, yet here their number was extraordinarily fluctuating. In some cases only comparatively few bacilli, and those exclusively in the giant cells of the "perlsucht" knots, were found, similarly as in scrofulous glands, and in the already mentioned caseous (cheesy) herds in the lungs of cattle. I am, therefore, not able to share the often-expressed opinion that "perlsucht" knots, in contract with the tubercles in man, are always rich in bacilli. Besides such cases as run their course slowly and always show very few bacilli, there are those in which permanently or only temporarily the number of bacilli may be very considerable.

Also, in the same lung bacilli may be found to be very numerous in some spots and very scarce in others. Sections prepared from large and hard, therefore older knots contained often only scattered bacilli in giant cells. The younger knots, on the contrary, showed themselves extraordinarily rich in bacilli and allowed the recognition of the formerly mentioned relations between bacilli and giant cells with great ease.

Besides this, bacilli are found between the small cells in such numbers that in places they give the specimen a bluish color.

The caseous mesenteric glands of cattle suffering from "perlsucht", which I received for examination, were always extraordinarily rich in bacilli. The bacilli were, on the contrary, less numerous in the ragged "perlsüchtigen" luxuriant growths, permeated with many little hard knots and taken from the pericardium of a beef-creature and also in the knots, which in such a case had their seat in the kidneys. In all the number of cases of "perlsucht" examined amounted to seventeen, and the bacilli were wanting in none of them.

2.—TUBERCULOSIS OF THE HORSE.

Four cases, of which, to be sure, I could not obtain all the organs, were examined, nevertheless it could easily be seen that tuberculosis of the horse takes a middle place between that of cattle and the same disease in man. In places the tuberculous formations on the peritoneum and omentum bore the greatest resemblance to the "perlsucht"-knots of cattle, while in the same cases and simultaneously, the lungs were permeated with extraordinarily numerous miliary tubercles, which give them, on the surface of the section completely, the appearance of a human lung supplied with miliary tubercles. In one case the way in which the tuberculous virus had got into the course of the blood led to miliary tuberculosis. Namely, the retroperitoneal glands were, cha:.ged into a very large tumor permeated with firm yellowish caseous herds, which partly enclosed the vena cava inferior and formed uneven protuberances towards the interior of the ven. Sections through this gland mass, and especially through the knots reaching into the vena cava, exhibited extraordinary numbers of tuberculous bacilli, partly free, partly filling the numerous giant cells. Several of the knots were softened on their surface and had plainly mingled many tuberculous bacill with the blood of the vena cava. The miliary tuberculosis had, therefore, arisen here in the same manner as it has been shown by Weigert to arise in man.

Also, in the other cases of tuberculosis in horses, tuberculous bacilli could be proved in the knots from the omentum and peritoneum, in the immensely enlarged bronchial glands, and in the tuberculous knots of the lungs, spleen and liver; and moreover, here and there they were discovered in great numbers.

3.—TUBEROULOSIS OF THE PIG.

This appears to occur comparatively very often. Especially there are often found in the pig, caseous changes in the lymph glands of the neck which are of a tuberculous nature. In four cases in which I received such glands for examination, tuberculous bacilli were found each time, partly free, partly in giant cells. Besides this there occurs in a pig a peculiar form of caseous pneumonia, in which large parts of the lung are lobularly infiltrated with greyish-red to greyish-yellow colored masses and are almost completely empty of air. I have examined five cases of this form. The alveoli were here and there filled with dense heaps of tuberculous bacilli. In other places the bacilli had already forced themselves into the surrounding tissue and bacilli-bearing giant cells had formed here. In two cases one or even several bacilli-bearing giant cells frequently showed themselves free in the alveolar spaces. It here concerned itself plainly in all these cases of caseous pneumonia about a tuberculosis arising from the aspiration of considerable masses of bacilli. In one case the still fresh infection of the lung appeared to have proceeded from the tonsils, which were changed into deep ulcerations provided with a caseous base and also containing tuberculous bacilli. Once I received pieces of muscle from a pig, which were impregnated with numerous little knots for the most part calcareous. These proved themselves under microscopic examination to be tuberculous; they contained giant cells, supplied with tuberculous bacilli.

4.—TUBERCULOSIS OF THE GOAT AND SHEEP.

I only once had opportunity to examine a lung of a sheep supplied with tuberculous knots and the bronchial glands belonging with it partly caseous and calcerous. The lung tubercles contained giant cells, with not very numerous tuberculous bacilli. In the bronchial glands the bacilli were present more abundantly. One case from the goat was also at my disposal, which, to be sure, had special interest, in so far that a cavity almost as large as a fist had formed in the right as well as in the left lung, and furnished the proof that under some circumstances a condition completely analogous to human phthisis can be developed in animals. The cavities were partly filled with caseous pus. Their inner wall was sinuous, raw and fringy. Numerous giant cells with tuberculous bacilli were found in the enclosing tissue; single bacilli could also be shown in the purulent contents of the cavities. Besides this, the lung tissue in the surroundings of the cavities and for a pretty wide space was impregnated with miliary tuberculous knots, which were also provided with bacilli-bearing giant cells. Some largish knots in the spleen and liver, as well as the greatly enlarged and caseous bronchial glands, showed the same behavior.

5.—TUBERCULOSIS OF THE FOWL.

This is usually endemic and not seldom destroys all the fowls of a yard. More or less rough, sometimes also perfectly smooth tumors are found in the intestines and liver of the diseased animals. These tumors are as large as peas or walnuts. In one of the cases examined one knot in the liver even reached the size of a little apple. These tumors are of a compact constitution, show themselves spotted whitish and yellowish on the intersection, and on the yellow spots are partly calcareous. In one case tuberculous knots of almost the size of a hemp-seed were present in the marrow of the bone of the long tubes (röhren). All these knots, which belong to four different creatures, were extraordinarily rich in tuberculous bacilli, these heaping themselves especially in the immediate surroundings of the calcarous parts. In the knots situated on the intestines the tuberculous bacilli could be followed into the villi intestinalis, and it is hence not improbable that they found their entrance to the inner organs from the intestines, especially also as once only scattered little knots were found in the lungs. On the other hand, it may be concluded from this result, that the bacilli can get into the contents of the intestines, be excreted with these and give rise to further infection, just as is the case in intestinal tuberculosis in man.

TUBERCULOSIS OF THE MONKEY.

In the case of the monkey tuberculosis acts differently, in several respects, from the tuberculosis in man. It does not usually remain confined long to one organ, but at an early stage spreads itself over the whole body. Then it does not appear in the form of numerous little knots, which have an equal size, as in human miliary tuberculosis, but leads to the formation of a larger or smaller number of tuberculous herds, whose size is very varying and which contain, especially in the liver, spleen and glands, instead of the firm caseous substance of the tuberculosis in man, a rather thinly fluid pus, so that they rather make the impression of multiple abscesses than of tubercles. Beside these, to be sure, the typical forms of the grey tubercle with the yellowish centre occur in the lungs, on the pleura and the omentum. But these are also of various sizes and one gains the impression that the spread of the tuberculous virus in the monkey does not take place all at once, as in miliary tuberculosis in man, but is continuous and only in small quantities.

The number of tuberculous monkeys examined by me amounts to eight. In all these the disease had risen spontaneously, and apparently the first infectious herd still existed in the lung. Only in one case had the tuberculosis proceeded from the cavitas navium. An abscess had formed in the nasal duct, which was probably caused by a wound from a scratch at the entrance of the nose, and had spread constantly but slowly farther upon the septum and the turbinated bones. The submaxilary lymph-glands swelled and became purulent. Not until then did the previously active and strong animal have trouble in breathing and become emaciated. In the dissection very numerous tubercles of varying size were found in the lung, spleen, liver and omentum.

In all the cases the tuberculous bacilli could be proved, and, moreover, in the tubercles of the most different organs. Nevertheless the number of bacilli was not very large.

7.—Spontaneous Tuberculosis of Guinea Pigs and Rabbits.

Among many hundred rabbits and guinea pigs, which were bought for experimental purposes, were experimentally used and were finally dissected, there was not a single animal which was tuberculous. Not until after the attemp's at infection with tuberculous substances had begun and a large number of tuberculous animals found themselves in separate cages, but in the same room with other animals, single cases of spontaneous tuberculosis occurred among the latter. Nevertheless plainly visible symptoms of tuberculosis hardly ever showed themselves in such animals until they had spent three to four months in a room with tuberculous animals. It was a very characteristic appearance also, that when the number of artificially infected tuberculous animals decreased, the cases of spontaneous tuberculosis became correspondingly rare; the reverse being also true. For a considerable time, when only very few tuberculous animals were kept in the space used for such experiments, the spontaneous tuberculosis among the other very numerous guinea pigs and rabbits ceased entirely. The changes which were found in the animals dying from spontaneous tuberculosis distinguish themselves from those caused by artificial infection in a very characteristic manner, so that the varying methods of infection can be recognized with all certainty. There were regularly in animals dying with spontaneous tuberculosis one or more large tuberculous herds in the lungs, which were far advanced in caseous degeneration and at the same time decidedly enlarged and caseous bronchial glands. A few times larger herds were wanting in the lungs, only the bronchial glands were extraordinarily large and filled with caseous contents. The tuberculous changes had made in the other organs comparatively little progress.

The artificially infected animals conducted themselves differently according as they were infected by subcutaneous inoculation or by the inhalation of bacilli-bearing liquids. Usually the inoculation took place in one side of the belly, and the lymph-glands situated next to the point of inoculation were found considerably swollen and caseous. The bronchial glands, on the contrary, were almost always so small that they could scarcely be found. Also in these cases the liver and spleen had undergone the greatest tuberculous changes, while the tubercles in the lungs were still comparatively small. In the case of animals infected by inhalation, which had always taken considerable numbers of bacilli into the lungs, there were found corresponding to this, not one or a few great herds, but a very large number of little tubercles in the lungs. If one considers these experiences gained from artificially infected animals, then he will be obliged to represent to himself the spontaneous tuberculosis, as it occurred under the above mentioned circumstances in guinea pigs and rabbits, as having arisen through inhalation of one or more infectious germs, that is bacilli.

Of this sort of spontaneously-diseased animals I have examined seventeen guinea pigs and eight rabbits, among them a wild rabbit, which, as the only one of ten animals of the same sort, died after three months' imprisonment, tuberculous in a high degree. These all had many, in some cases indeed extraordinarily numerous bacilli in the surroundings of the caseous herds of the lungs. In the secondarily arisen tubercles the number of bacilli was usually less. It seems to me worthy of mention, that many times, in the larger caseous herds of the lungs, the central dissolution was very far advanced, and in consequence of the same complete cavities, though of slight extent, had formed. Up to a certain degree spontaneous-inhalation-tuberculosis brings on conditions in these animals which are analogous to those of human phthisis. The infection only does not remain long enough localized, it spreads too early to other regions of the body and leads thereby to the death of the animal before important cavities can form as they occur in the human lung.

Tuberculosis of the remaining organs takes a very peculiar course in both the rabbit and the guinea pig, and moreover a different one in each. In the beginning, in both sorts of animals, the tuberculous knots in the liver and spleen have the usual characteristic appearance which they maintain in the lungs. They are miliary, gray looking little knots, with yellowish centre, and of a quite compact consistence. In guinea pigs the spleen is decidedly enlarged, and of a blackish-red color, on which background the grayish knots show very plainly. Very soon, however, the tubercles become confluent and there arise larger whitish gray islands. These too increase constantly and give the spleen a light grayish-red and blackish-red marbled appearance. Finally the light parts get the upper hand, and the spleen can then take a wholly unusual appearance, which does not in the least suggest the origin of this condition in tuberculosis, especially when it comes to little ruptures and hemorrhages in the fragile spleen-substance, by which it gets a still gayer coloring. At all events it is very peculiar that tuberculosis in the spleen of the guinea pig leads to such widespread "congulation-necrosis," but never to genuine caseous degeneration, while in the lymph-glands of these animals a decided caseous degeneration occurs. The liver of the guinea pig acts in an exactly similar manner. In the first place gray disseminated knots form, lighter parts appear, which increase, become confluent, and become intensely yellow in color. The liver increases enormously in size, and finally looks marbled, with spots of yellow and brown. In the darker parts of the liver there are usually still fresh grey little knots to be seen.

In the dissection of a guinea pig tuberculous in a high degree, beside the lungs permeated with little grey knots, the spleen, immensely enlarged and marbled with light grey and blackish-grey, and the liver also decidedely enlarged and marbled in brown and yellow, attract the eye, and it gives a total which can be mistaken for no other disease occurring in these animals. By the microscopic investigation of a spleen or liver so changed it is shown that in the ligh colored parts no nucleus coloring occurs; the cells have died and indeed a sort of "coagulation-necrosis" is present. A large part of the organ is dead, but no further dissolution occurs, the organ keeps its form and has only changed its color. In these dead masses usually only scattered bacilli are to be found. Only in single cases I have seen a peculiar increase and arrangement of the bacilli in the necrotic liver tissue, of which I will speak later. The bacilli occur more or less numerously on the border of the necrotic parts, and are then frequently enclosed by giant cells.

In the kidneys of guinea pigs I have never observed tubercles visible to the naked eye.

In rabbits the spleen and liver also appear enlarged, though in a far less degree than in guinea pigs. In this animal the tubercles always remain small and insignificant in the organs named, and there are never such changes as were described in the case of guinea pigs. On the contrary, the kidneys are almost always supplied with a number of whitish knots, which grow to the size of peas. In these knots the tuberculous bacilli are usually found in abundance, and mostly arranged in nests. Sometimes also I have found urethræ which were filled with bacilli.

8.—ARTIFICIALLY GENERATED TUBERCULOSIS IN ANIMALS.

Artificially generated tuberculosis conducts itself in general just like that which arises spontaneously. It takes also the form characteristic of every special species of animals, and in fowls, for example, leads to the development of compact, knotty tumors on the intestines and the liver; in rabbits to the formation of small gray tubercles with yellowish centre in lungs and spleen, and larger whitish knots in the kidneys; and in guinea pigs causes the considerable enlargement of the spleen and liver, together with the peculiar gray or yellow marbled coloring of these organs.

Of course the various sorts of infection condition certain differences in the course of the tuberculosis in the form of the pathological changes. It is of the greatest significance whether the infection was brought about with very few bacilli or with greater numbers of them. The distinction conditioned upon this may be studied most simply in the eye of the rabbit. Namely, if as few bacilli as possible be put into the anterior eye-chamber there arise first separate little gray knots, genuine miliary tubercles, which become yellowish in the centre. Their number increases gradually, they finally become confluent and not until after a considerable time do they lead to the general caseous degeneration and destruction of the eye as well as to the appearance of tubercles in other organs. When, on the contrary, from the beginning an abundant number of bacilli is introduced into the eye-chamber, the first step is not the formation of single little knots, but the same appearance is manifest which has already been cursorily mentioned in the description of lung phthisis as diffuse caseous infiltration, after the aspiration of substances rich in bacilli. Also in this case the eye becomes diffusely caseously infiltrated, perishes very quickly, and the general infection, the appearance of many little gray knots in the spleen and lungs, takes place very early, usually after three weeks.

Almost the same distinction in the effect of infectious masses poor or rich in bacilli is manifest when the same are put into the abdominal cavity of guinea pigs; the one time disseminated tuberculous knots of the peritoneum and omentum with slow progress of the process, the other time considerable thickening, shrinking, and caseous degeneration of the omentum, together with a diffused infiltration of the peritoneum, with numberless tuberculous knots of the smallest kind.

The relations are still different when the bacilli are brought directly into the course of the blood, when they reach the lungs in considerable quantities by inhalation, or when the infection occurs only from a small wound on some part of the body. In each of these cases the first stages of the changes must correspond with the mode of infection used in each case.

But in its further course the disease always takes the type of tuberculosis. Especially, the secondary tuberculous knots arising at a distance from the original spot of infection always bear one and the same character. They are in the beginning little gray knots consisting of herds of epithelioid cells, contain giant cells and tuberculous bacilli exactly like the tuberculous knots arising spontaneously, from which they are in no wise distinguished.

A special description of the conduct of the tuberculous bacilli in artificially generated tuberculosis is therefore not needed, and I can limit myself to the summary enumeration of the cases examined. These concern 273 guinea pigs, 105 rabbits, 3 dogs, 13 cats, 2 German marmots, 10 domestic fowls, 12 pigeons, 28 white mice (variety of the house mouse), 44 field mice (arvicola arvalis), 19 rats.

In these animals tuberculous bacilli were found in the tubercles without exception. On account of the great number of animals it was, to be sure, not possible to examine all the organs provided with tubercles in every separate case, and I have been obliged in most cases to prove the presence of bacilli by crushing and spreading out some tuberculous knots from the lungs or spleen on covering glasses.

If, now, the result of the microscopic investigation of tuberculous objects, as it has been minutely described in the above, be summarized, we have the following results:

In all those disease processes which, by their course as well as by their characteristic microscopic structure and the infectious qualities of their products, must be considered as genuine tuberculosis, there occur regularly in the tuberculous herds staff-shaped forms, whose presence can be proved with the help of special methods of coloring. This is the case as well in tuberculosis of man as in that of animals of the various sorts. Also the number of single cases which generally and specially were examined for the individual forms of tuberculosis is large enough to maintain that here the question is not one of an occasional but of a constant appearance, and that therefore tuberculous bacilli are among the component parts typical of the tubercles and their products. The two single cases in which bacilli were not to be found concern the microscopic investigation of the pus of a tuberculous abscess of the kidneys and the pus from the abscess of a vortex caries. That the bacilli were really wanting in these cases can nevertheless not be maintained, because here just such products of tuberculosis were examined as are almost regularly to be found without bacilli, owing to the fact that those originally present had vanished, as has been shown in the other examinations. Without doubt bacilli would have been found in these cases also if the original spots from which the pus came could have been examined.

On the contrary, until now, however manifold the examinations of the most various disease processes in men and animals, the bacilli peculiar to tuberculosis have never been found in other diseases. Where this has been said to be the case the statements have proved themselves erroneous, proceeding from a wrong use of the methods of examination.

A second important result is that the appearance of tuberculous bacilli marks the beginning of the tuberculous process. They appear just when the first changes in the cell elements of the tissue are noticeable. Not until the tuberculous bacilli are present do the heaps of epithelioid cells, the formation of giant cells, and the especially characteristic caseous products arising from the perishing of these cell elements, appear. Further, the presence and the number of the tuberculous bacilli are in closest connection with the progress of the tuberculous process. For where the tuberculosis bears a chronic character, only few and scattered bacilli are found; where, on the contrary, it is making rapid progress, numerous and thickly heaped bacilli are present; and where the tuberculous process has come to a standstill or has run its course, the bacilli vanish.

These three facts, namely, that the tuberculous bacilli occur regularly and exclusively in tuberculosis; that they in time and place precede all the peculiar pathological changes of tuberculosis; and that their number and their appearance and disappearance stand in direct relation to the course of tuberculosis—these facts allow us to conclude with great probability that tuberculous bacilli are not an accidental accompaniment of tuberculosis, but stand in an original connection with it.

Such far-reaching consequences hang on the decision of this question, that one cannot rest in having brought it near to a solution, but must make the attempt to decide it with undeniable certainty. Moreover, a further investigation of the conditions of life and development of these parasites promised further important light on the ætiology of tuberculosis and on the ways and means of defending humanity against this most destructive disease.

The only possibility of reaching this goal lay in taking the same way which had approved itself for the investigation of other bacteria diseases. The tuberculous bacilli must be isolated from the diseased organs, bred outside of the body in "reinculturen" (pure cultures), their behavior in this way investigated, and finally tuberculosis be artificially generated by such bacilli, freed from all admixture with the disease products.

II.—ISOLATION AND REINCULTUREN OF TUBERCULOUS BACILLI.

It could be seen in advance that the obtaining of reinculturen of tuberculous bacilli would be attended with difficulties, and therefore from the beginning the method of culture upon firm, transparent breeding ground was adopted, because this is superior to all other methods of reinculturen in certainty and ease of management. With reference to the principle which lies at the foundation of this method, as well as in regard to its difference from other treatment, and the manifold advantages which it offers, I would refer to the minute description of the same given in the earlier pages of this paper.

At first it was attempted to grow the bacilli from crushed lung tubercles on "nahrgelatine" (meat-water-pepton-gelatine), but without success. These attempts had been made in the temperature of the room, because in greater heat the gelatine becomes liquid and thereby loses all the advantages of a firm breeding ground. Since it seemed probable that the attempts failed because a temperature of 20° C. was not sufficient for the growth of the bacilli, it was necessary to supply another firm, and at the same time transparent, breeding ground, which should contain all the component parts demanded for the nourishment of bacilli. Such an one seemed to offer itself in stiffened blood serum. I had found in experiments made for the purpose of sterilizing blood serum by repeated warming, according to the method first given by Tyndall for hay-infusion, that the serum when warmed for a considerable time over 65° C., remained stiffened and transparent. Such a breeding ground can be exposed for a considerable time to temperatures which correspond with the temperature of the body, without undergoing any changes. Bacilli-bearing substances were spread out on such stiffened transparent blood-serum, and left in a breeding apparatus at 37° C. The direct examination frequently undertaken under slight magnifying power showed after some days the appearance of peculiarly shaped colonies, which, as was recognized under a stronger magnifying power, and with the use of color reaction, consisted only of tuberculous bacilli. Nevertheless, before I proceed to the more exact description of these bacilli cultures, I have still to describe the preparation of the stiffened blood serum, which in course of time has proved itself to be the most practical.

Even the flowing of the blood into the necessary vessels demands several prudential measures. As vessels for catching the blood rather high cylindrical glasses provided with a glass stopper are suitable. These are well cleaned, then washed out with a one per cent. sublimate solution, in order to kill any bacteria germs possibly clinging to them, and then washed again with alcohol to remove the sublimate. Then one lets the blood of the slaughtered animal flow immediately from the cut into these purified vessels. Nevertheless it is well not to catch the blood first flowing after the stab, because it carries away with it cut hairs and particles of dirt from the skin and fur. The vessel should be filled nearly to the rim, closed with a stopper and placed immediately in a refrigerator. As soon as the coagulation of the blood begins the vessel must be kept perfectly still, as otherwise the formation of a firm cruor would be disturbed and a quantity of red blood-corpuscles would be mixed with the serum. The blood-filled vessels remain in the refrigerator from twenty-four to thirty hours and even longer, until a good-sized layer of completely transparent amber yellow serum has formed over the cruor. When the serum is colored more or less bloody, then it contains too many red blood-corpuscles and becomes opaque in warming. The serum is now filled by means of a pipette into re-agent glasses which are provided with a wadding stopper. The pipette as well as the re-agent glasses and the wadding stopper, are previously made free from bacteria germs by heating them at least an hour at 150–160° C. in a double walled heating box made of sheet iron. One fills the re-agent glasses about one-third with serum, and closes them immediately with a stopper made of cotton wadding. In spite of all this care there are regularly found in the blood serum bacteria germs, which come from the air, from the hair of the slaughtered animal, etc., and would very soon cause decay and decomposition of the serum if they were not destroyed. Other liquids destined for the "reincultur" of bacteria can be sterilized, that is made free from all bacteria germs, easily and certainly by boiling. This cannot be done in the case of blood serum, because by higher temperature it completely loses its transparency. There remains, therefore, only the method adopted by Tyndall in the sterilization of hay-infusion, that is, instead of heating it once to a boiling temperature, to heat it repeatedly at a temperature of 55°–60°. The bacteria, namely, if not spore-bearing, are easily killed in liquids even by a temperature of 55°. The spores, on the contrary, as is well known, endure these temperatures and do not die until the boiling point is reached. Once heating of the liquid, therefore, only kills the spore-free bacteria and leaves the spores which may be there untouched. In the medium so favorable to their growth, however, the spores germinate soon, changing themselves into bacilli, and as such cannot stand a temperature of 55° they are therefore killed by successive warmings before they have had time to form new spores. But since the spores germinate at different times, and often do not develop into bacilli until after several days, it is necessary to repeat the warming. Experience has taught that it is almost always sufficient to warm the blood serum for an hour for five successive days to free it completely from germs which are capable of development. This warming can take place in an open water bath. It is safer to use a tin vessel especially kept for the purpose and which possesses double walls filled with water and a cover constructed in the same manner, so that the warming shall be equal on all sides.

The blood serum sterilized in this manner is then stiffened, and in order to get the greatest possible surface for inoculation the re-agent glasses should be held in a very slanting position. Also tin boxes with a double bottom and a glass cover, placed in a slanting position, are practical for this purpose. The water in the bottom of the glass is so heated that a thermometer lying in the box between the re-agent glasses shows 65° C. In this temperature the serum stiffens in from half an hour to an hour. The serum of different animals is not uniform in its conduct. The serum of sheep usually stiffens most quickly, calf serum most slowly. When serum is warmed at a higher temperature, for example at 70°, it stiffens far more quickly, but it is then more difficult to keep it transparent. A well-prepared blood serum must be almost completely clear, transparent and amber-like. At most only at the lower end of the re-agent glass and in the thickest layer may it be whiter and less transparent. It must also not be too soft, but must almost have the consistence of a hard-boiled hen's egg.

During the warming, usually on the upper cooler wall of the re-agent glass, more or less steam condenses and forms drops which, when the re-agent glass is taken up flow down and collect between the deepest part of the serum and of the glass wall. A small part of the area of inoculation is covered by this liquid. Nevertheless the liquid is in so far of value that it takes up by diffusion soluble substances from the stiffened blood serum and is changed into a very good breeding solution. When the bacteria to be cultivated are spread out upon the stiffened serum, just up to the edge of this liquid, then they develop at the same time and close by each other on the firm breeding ground and in the breeding liquid, so that their special modes of growth in liquid and upon a firm substratum can be immediately compared.

When the re-agent glasses provided with stiffened blood serum are preserved for a length of time, since the wadding stopper does not prevent evaporation of the moisture, a very gradual drying of the serum, progressing from above downwards, takes place, yet it occurs so slowly that for months a sufficiently large area suitable for cultures remains at disposal between the upper dried part of the serum and the lower part covered by the liquid.

When the sterilization of the blood serum has not succeeded, this shows itself a few days after the stiffening, especially if the serum be put experimentally into the breeding apparatus. In these cases little whitish points form which appear singly or in larger numbers, and soon enlarge. Sometimes the blood serum becomes liquid under the influence of such bacteria, then loses its clearness and becomes covered with a whitish skin. Microscopic investigation shows that we here always have bacilli which plainly have proceeded from spores germinating late. As a matter of course, only such serum glasses may be used for "reinculturen" as after several days' stay in the breeding apparatus show no trace of such impurities, but remain completely clear and transparent. For many purposes, especially when it is wished to examine the reinculturen directly with the microscope under slight magnifying power, it is to the purpose to stiffen the serum in watch glasses or other suitable vessels. Such vessels should have a glass cover as a protection against the entrance of air germs. They are further placed in glass vessels which are lined with moist blotting paper, and can so be exposed to the breeding temperature. So sure a protection from injurious impurities as the re-agent glasses closed by wadding is, to be sure, not given by this arrangement, and reinculturen continued through many repeated breedings of tuberculous bacilli are only to be carried on by the help of blood serum stiffened in the re-agent glasses.

Just as great care as the preparation of the sterilized stiffened blood serum demands is absolutely necessary when the sowing is to be made on the prepared breeding ground, if at the same time the entrance of foreign germs and the defilement of the breeding ground by bacteria and fungi is to be prevented.

As to the material to be used for sowing, that is naturally the most suitable which contains many bacilli, is of a soft nature (that the bacilli may be spread as quickly as possible), and is as fresh as possible, that is as free from the bacteria of decay. When these latter are confined to the surface of the organ which is to serve as a point of departure for culturen, it is still possible with certain precautions to obtain reinculturen of tuberculous bacilli. But as soon as the foreign bacteria have forced themselves into the deeper layers all attempts to separate the tuberculous bacilli from them in culturen will be in vain, because the bacteria of decay grow with extraordinary rapidity in comparison with tuberculous bacilli and have taken possession of the entire breeding ground before the last have reached a visible growth.

Also, when the sowing material contains very few bacilli and is of a firm consistence, there are difficulties in causing the cultures to grow. In this case, namely, the bacill-bearing substance cannot be so crushed that the bacilli can be spread out free and upon the surface of the blood serum ; on this account they remain hidden in the substance, develop there and the colonies growing in scanty **numbers** withdraw themselves easily from observation.

The **reinculturen** succeed most surely when a tubercle rich in bacilli, or richly tuberculous substance from **the** interior of a still slightly caseous lymphgland of a guinea pig killed for the purpose, be used for sowing. For this purpose one should proceed in the following manner : A number of knives, scissors and pincettes are so thoroughly heated in **the flame that they are freed from** all bacteria clinging to them, and laid ready in **such a manner that** no impurities can afterward get at them. In the mean time, the animal, which must **just have been** killed, is spread out upon a dissecting board. In order, when cutting through the skin to avoid dusting **off** particles of dirt, hairs, etc., the fur of the animal should be thoroughly moistened with **a** one per cent. strong sublimate solution. After this one cuts through the skin with the still hot scissors and with the help of the still hot pincette, and lays it back on both sides so far that the lymph-glands of the regio axillaris and inguinalis are completely free, but the glands, if they are to be used for reinculturen, must not be touched with the instruments used in cutting the skin. With another hot pair of scissors another piece, 1-2 qu. ctm. large, is cut out from the side wall of the thorax, and the surface of the lungs laid bare. By this means a number of little tuberculous knots are made accessible, from which, as quickly as possible, with still other instruments, which must have been cooled for this operation, one or more are prepared. In order to free the bacilli contained in the little knots, one cuts or crushes these with the scissors or, still better, between two scalpels which have been previously heated and cooled. The substance broken and rubbed to **pieces** is then put into the re-agent glass, spread out upon the surface and rubbed with a platinum wire which has been melted into a glass staff, and has immediately before using been heated and cooled again. The re-agent glass is to be held slantingly or almost horizontally between the thumb and the forefinger, and the wadding cork must be so held in the mean time with the other fingers of the hand that impurities from coming in contact with other objects may not reach it. The placing of the substance on the stiffened serum which, for the sake of brevity may be called inoculation, must be done as quickly as possible in order that the germs of foreign organisms from the air may not get upon the inoculating substance, or into the re-agent glass. It is also advisable to undertake the experiment in a room in which no dust is stirred up, and moreover all unnecessary motions which ould cause dust from clothes, etc., to get into the air are to be avoided, since experience has taught that the germs of micro-organisms cling to the particles of dust suspended in the air.

In spite of all these prudential measures the entrance of single foreign germs is not to be avoided with absolute certainty, and it is necessary in every single case to inoculate several re-agent glasses, perhaps 5-10, that if the reincultur does not succeed in the one or the other, the remainder may be free from all impurities.

In such manner as the preparation of lung tubercles for sowing has been described, must the experiments be conducted when lymph-glands, tubercles of the spleen, etc., are to be used for culturen. One must always operate with instruments that have been made red-hot, and these must be changed every time a new layer is to be exposed. All preparatory cuts which do not touch the inoculating substance itself are to be made with hot instruments, the inoculating mass on the contrary to be cut out with cooled scissors and pincette. The constant change of instruments is necessary in order that impurities which might attach themselves to the instruments in cutting the skin and the superficial layers may not be carried into the culturen.

When the organs of animals which have just died or just been killed were at my disposal, and the sowing was carried on in the manner just described with substances containing tuberculous bacilli, the reinculturen have succeeded without exception. The result was, on the contrary, uncertain when the material from human corpses or cattle suffering from "perlsucht" was used, since there were always impurities on the surface, and it was moreover not wholly fresh when I received it. In these cases I have first repeatedly and thoroughly washed the surface of the object with one per cent. sublimate solution, then with constantly changed, glowing hot instruments taken off the upper layers one at a time, and cut the inoculating substance from a depth at which I could feel sure it was free from foreign bacteria. In this manner I usually succeeded in obtaining reinculturen from material of this sort, especially from little lung vomicæ lying near the surface whose covering was removed with hot instruments after treatment with sublimate.

After the stiffened serum is inoculated with a bacilli-bearing substance, the vessels are placed in a breeding apparatus and kept constantly at a temperature of 37° C. Not every breeding apparatus is adapted to the culture of tuberculous bacilli. The growth proceeds but slowly and the vessels must therefore remain for weeks at a time in the apparatus. When the breeding apparatus, owing to its construction, causes a rapid evaporation of liquid from the vessels, the serum dries before the tuberculous bacilli have developed into visible colonies. Especially such apparatus as are unequally warmed, so that the steam always present in them condenses on the cooler places, for example on the glass cover, and must be constantly replaced by steam developed from the culturen vessels, cannot be used. The Arsonval thermostaten are very practical; the warmth is evenly divided and the serum keeps almost unchanged in them.

In the first few days one will notice no change in the culturen in the breeding apparatus. If a change occurs, if whitish or even other colored drops or spots appear on the surface of the serum, if these enlarge more or less quickly, becloud the liquid in the bottom of the glass, or even liquefy the serum, this is a sign that the cultur is not successful, and that foreign bacteria have forced themselves in and grown more luxuriantly than the bacilli. If one examines such drops or spots he always finds them to consist of bacilli or micrococci which, under Ehrlich's color treatment, always take a color opposite to that of the tuberculous bacilli, and are distinguished from them in size and shape.

In those little glasses which have remained free from such impurities the first suggestions of the growing colonies of tuberculous bacilli do not show themselves until after ten to fifteen days. They appear as pale white little points or spots, which lie on the surface of the serum, are without lustre, and on that account show plainly against their moist surroundings. They can best be compared with little dry scales which are slightly attached to the serum surface. According as the inoculating substance was rubbed upon a greater or less surface, and according to the abundance of bacilli in the same, the scales develop in smaller or greater numbers and extent on the serum surface.

The single scales only reach a limited spread, so that when only a few are present they remain separated. When numerous and thickly crowded together, on the contrary, they finally unite and form a thin, grayish white lustreless coating on the serum.

A very different image is presented by the cultures developing from substances which contain only scattered bacilli. As has already been suggested, one does not succeed in such cases in freeing the bacilli by rubbing and crushing the substance, and spreading it on the surface of the serum. They remain, in the substance and form there colonies which grow almost to the size of a poppy seed. In such cases there can be no doubt that each single little colony proceeded from one single, or at most two bacilli, because microscopic investigation has always found only 1–2 bacilli in a giant cell of the tissue in question. Accordingly we can also further conclude that, in the formerly mentioned examples, the single scales developing upon the serum proceeded also from single bacilli.

If a beginning of reinoculatures of tuberculous bacilli has been obtained in the manner just described, they can be carried on without difficulty. For this purpose some of the whitish scales can be put into a re-agent glass containing stiffened serum by means of the platinum wire, which must be made glowing hot and then cooled again, immediately before its use. By the use of this wire the scales are also to be spread as much as possible on the serum surface, and rubbed to pieces. In this second sowing far more numerous bacilli reach the serum surface, and can there be spread more easily and evenly than was the case with the original inoculating material; in consequence of which one obtains in this and later breedings, no longer single scales, but coherent, membrane-like colonies. These take in general the figure which the motions of the platinum wire prescribed beforehand in the sowing. They can therefore be laid on in lines, either in a perpendicular or horizontal direction, or may take any figure one may choose to construct on the serum. Vigorously growing cultures nevertheless spread more or less beyond the original limits of the sowing. This spread is, however, not the consequence of independent motions of the bacilli, which, as already shown, they do not possess, but it takes place in consequence of the fact that in the constant increase of the bacilli the increase of mass does not take place in the diameter of the thickness, but in area. The growing bacilli do not heap themselves upon each other, but have the tendency to spread out in area and push the already formed coherent membrane away over the surface of the serum. This is most marked when the bacilli membrane reaches the liquid at the base of the re-agent glass. It does not penetrate into the liquid, but it forces itself over the same and forms a fine cover on the surface of the liquid. Very often indeed it presses up to a height of some millimeters on the opposite side of the glass.

The bacilli "cultures" have other noteworthy qualities by which they may be distinguished from other bacteria "cultures" by the naked eye. In the first place, they never liquify the serum, as **some sorts of** bacteria regularly do. They do not penetrate into the serum, but always remain on its surface and lie loosely there. In consequence of this the membrane-like bacilli vegetation can be lifted and washed away by tipping the re-agent glass so that the liquid at its base may flow over the surface of the **serum**. Other bacteria possess a pap-like consistence and let themselves mingle **with** the liquid, making them cloudy. This is not **the case with tuberculous** bacilli. The thin membranes formed by them do not dissolve **in the liquid, but** in consequence of their firm consistence **break** into larger **or smaller lumps, which** are washed away by the liquid, and finally collect at the bottom of the same. The peculiar stiff and brittle constitution of the colonies shows itself best in the part of the "cultur" which covers over the liquid in the re-agent glass. As soon as this liquid **is set in motion** the little skin on its surface breaks into plates and lumps, **which slowly sink to the bottom.** The liquid always remains clear, as well when the bacilli vegetation itself stretches over it, as **when by washing** off **of the** serum surface masses of bacilli get into it, **or when** in the beginning the inoculating substance is intentionally put into it. **From this** appearance also we should conclude, as direct observation had already shown, that the tuberculous bacilli possess no independent motion; for bacilli which **can move** disperse themselves in all directions through the breeding solutions, and give them **a** cloudy appearance.

Within certain limits, moreover, **the conduct of the** bacilli "culturen," as seen by the naked eye, **depends upon the consistence of the** blood **serum** upon which they grow. The firmer that is, the more the bacilli colonies have the constitution just described. On a **very soft gelatinous serum the development is** somewhat different. The distribution of the bacilli is not uniform because the **hard and firmly coherent masses of bacilli cannot be crushed on the soft serum in the sowing. The inoculating substance** therefore remains lying on **the serum in small detached crumbs. The** growth of the colonies does not reach so uniformly over the surface as on the **firm** serum, but leads to thicker compact masses which **cling firmly to the soft serum.** Even when the serum is somewhat less soft, so **that the colonies begin to spread** themselves out on the surface, one notices a **firmer attachment of the bacilli** membrane to the serum area. One does not then succeed in washing the membrane from the serum, or lifting it off with the platinum wire, without at the same time loosening parts of the serum.

When even the properties of the "culturen" noticeable with the naked eye show a difference from other bacteria and admit a judgment as to their purity, this is much more the case when they are examined under a moderately strong magnifying power, such as is obtained with Zeiss' Objective System, A.A., ocular 4, with drawn out tube, (80 **fold** magnifying power). **It is then seen that the bacilli colonies form** such peculiarly shaped figures as do no other sort of bacteria. **Microscopically of** course these colonies can be noticed far earlier than with the naked eye. **Already** five to six **days after** the sowing takes place and the "cultur" has been kept at breeding **warmth, peculiar, very dainty little figures appear on the surface** of the serum. These **appear as fine lines, often bow-shaped. The smallest have mostly the figure of an S. Longer colonies show the most manifold serpentine turns and windings which often** remind one of interlacing letters. While the ends of these lines run off into sharp points, in the middle they are more or less swollen to a spindle shape, and the smaller younger colonies are extraordinarily thin and delicate, the older thicker and of heavier forms. Gradually, by continued spreading and melting together, the windings take more and more a plate-like form which, by the ware-like designs and the transition of their borders into the peculiar oscillating lines of the single colonies, allow their origin as such to be recognized. Finally a number of such plates melt into each other, and form the previously described membrane-like bacilli colonies, while the plates proceeding from single colonies correspond with the whitish scales visible to the naked eye. In order to examine the colonies directly under the microscope and to follow their development, four-cornered little glass basins provided with a glass cover are specially adapted.

That these colonies are only formed by the tuberculous bacilli is soon seen when they are colored by Ehrlich's method, and examined by strong magnifying power. This can be done most practically when one presses a covering glass firmly to the surface of the serum covered with colonies and takes it up again. Numerous colonies then remain clinging to the covering glass in their natural arrangement and grouping, dry there and can be colored as was described formerly in the directions for covering glass specimens. The bacilli are not thrown together without method, but are placed with their axes of length parallel with the axis of length of colony. It is striking that the bacilli do not touch each other, but are separated, though only by slight spaces. As was formerly suggested, one may conclude from this conduct that the bacilli are surrounded by a building substance and are joined together by this, as is proved by the firm coherence of the colonies. Very frequently in farther advanced colonies one finds all or nearly all the bacilli spore-bearing.

Usually the "culturen" have reached the maximum of their development after four weeks and then remain unchanged. The continuation of the same is most practically carried on in intervals of from two to four weeks. Nevertheless such "culturen" as have existed for months are still capable of development and can be used for further breeding. By the method described in the above I have gained a number of reinculturen of tuberculous bacilli from different materials, and have continued them through a longer or shorter succession of breedings. Several attempts at "culturen," and indeed the first which were made, proceeded from guinea-pigs, which were tuberculously infected by inoculation from man and from various animals. Other "culturen" have been obtained directly from the original tuberculous material. The reinculturen indirectly gained by the help of the original inoculation of guinea-pigs relate to the following cases :

1.—Human lung-phthisis cultivated through twenty-two months, therefore almost two years, in thirty-four successive breedings ;

2.—Human lung-phthisis (caseous mass from the lung) cultivated for two and one-half months in five successive breedings ;

3.—Human lung-phthisis (contents of the lung cavity) cultivated for three months in six successive breedings ;

4.—Human miliary tuberculosis (tubercle of the lung) cultivated for seven months in twelve successive breedings ;

5.—Human miliary tuberculosis (tubercle of the pia mater) cultivated for three months in five successive breedings ;

6.—Human miliary tuberculosis (tubercle of the spleen) cultivated for two and one-half months in four successive breedings;

7.—Human tuberculosis of the uterus cultivated for four months in six successive breedings;

8.—Human intestinal tuberculosis (caseous mesentric glands) cultivated for six months in nine successive breedings;

9.—Human lung-phthisis (sputum) cultivated for four and one-half months in seven successive breedings;

10.—Scrofula in man (excised neck-gland) cultivated for seven months in twelve successive breedings;

11.—Tuberculosis in monkey (lung-tubercle) cultivated for six and one-half months in twelve successive breedings;

12.—Tuberculosis in monkey (tubercle of the spleen) cultivated for seven months in thirteen successive breedings;

13.—Tuberculosis in monkey (caseous bronchial glands) cultivated for four months in six successive breedings;

14.—Tuberculosis of cattle (pleura knots) cultivated for three months in five successive breedings;

15.—Tuberculosis of cattle (pleura knots) cultivated for three and one-half months in five successive breedings;

16.—Tuberculosis of cattle (peritoneal knots) cultivated for twenty-one months in twenty-nine successive breedings;

17.—Tuberculosis of cattle (peritoneal knots) cultivated for three months in five successive breedings;

18.—Tuberculosis of cattle (knots from the diaphragm) cultivated for four months in six successive breedings;

19.—Tuberculosis of cattle (pap-like caseous masses from the lung, first case) cultivated for eight months in thirteen successive breedings;

20.—Tuberculosis of cattle (pap-like caseous masses from the lung, second case) cultivated for three months in five successive breedings;

21.—Tuberculous bacilli "cultur" (Nos. 1 and 5 breeding) cultivated for four months in seven successive breedings;

The following reinculturen were obtained directly from the tuberculous material:

22.—Miliary tuberculosis from man (tubercle of the lung) cultivated for nineteen months in twenty-four successive breedings;

23.—Miliary tuberculosis from man (tubercle of the lung) cultivated for six months in ten successive breedings;

24.—Lung-phthisis from man (contents of a cavity) cultivated for seven months in eleven successive breedings;

25.—Lung-phthisis from man (contents of a little cavity in the tip of lungs) cultivated for eight months in ten successive breedings;

26.—Lung-phthisis of man (contents of a closed cavity) cultivated for eighteen months in twenty-four successive breedings;

27.—Caseous pneumonia of man (lung-tissue) cultivated for five months in seven successive breedings.

28.—Caseous pneumonia of man (lung tissue) cultivated for seven months in nine successive breedings;

29.—Scrofulous gland cultivated for six months in seven successive breedings ;

30.—Scrofulous gland cultivated for five months in seven successive breedings ;

31.—Scrofulous gland cultivated for three months in three successive breedings ;

32.—Scrofulous gland cultivated for three months in four successive breedings ;

33.—Tuberculous testicles cultivated for four months in six successive breedings :

34.—Fungous joint cultivated for fifteen months in nineteen successive breedings ;

35.—Lupus cultivated for sixteen months in twenty-one successive breedings ;

36.—Lung from cattle-tuberculosis (caseous mass) cultivated for six months in eight successive breedings ;

.—Lung from domestic animal tuberculosis (calcined knots) cultivated for five months in seven successive breedings ;

38.—Knots from the diaphragm of a tuberculously diseased domestic animal cultivated for nine months in fifteen successive breedings ;

39.—Knots from the pericardium of a tuberculously diseased domestic animal cultivated for eighteen months in twenty-three successive breedings ;

40.—Caseous pneumonia of the pig cultivated for five months in eight successive breedings ;

41.—Spontaneous tuberculosis of guinea pig (knots from the lungs) cultivated for six months in nine successive breedings ;

42.—Spontaneous tuberculosis of the guinea pig (spleen) cultivated for three months in five successive breedings ;

43.—Spontaneous tuberculosis of the guinea pig (knots from the lung) cultivated for four months in seven successive breedings.

The preservation of the culturen demands such an expenditure of time and trouble, that always only a certain number can be maintained at the same time. I let the most of them perish again as soon as their vegetative disease-producing qualities had been sufficiently established by a "culture" continued for several months, and by the inoculations undertaken with it. Only the Culturen No. 1 (lung-phthisis), No. 16 (tuberculosis of a domestic animal), No. 22 (miliary tuberculosis), No. 26 (contents of a cavity from a phthisical lung), No. 34 (fungous joint), No. 35 (lupus), No. 39 (tuberculosis of a domestic animal) have been continued until now, and are to be further preserved in order to find out whether in the life of the tuberculous bacilli continued outside of the animal body some sort of changes may not occur in their qualities. It might appear strange that comparatively so large a number of "culturen" were established, when a few would have sufficed for observing the conduct of the bacilli in the "culturen." Nevertheless in the beginning it appeared to me by no means impossible, that although the bacilli of the various tuberculous forms,—lupus, phthisis etc.—showed microscopically no difference, the bacilli derived from the various sources might perhaps manifest differences in the culturen. But in spite of the closest attention directed to this point, I have been able to find nothing of the kind. In the "culturen" also, whether taken from miliary tubercles or from the contents of vomicæ, often lupus, often tuberculosis of domestic animals, the tuberculous bacilli have been completely uniform in their conduct.   In no way has a change made itself noticed in the "culturen" continued for a longer period, between sixteen and twenty-two months.   If I formally made the claim that the culturen of tuberculous bacilli possess especially characteristic properties, by means of which the tuberculous bacilli could be distinguished from other bacteria, almost with greater certainty and certainly with more important grounds than by means of their tinctorial qualities, I can in confirmation of this claim appeal to a very rich amount of examined material.   There were, namely, after the favorable properties of the stiffened blood serum were recognized, numberless attempts made, partly from reinculturen of various bacteria, partly from the sowing of the most various animal substances on blood serum, but vegetations which resembled the culturen of tuberculous bacilli never appeared.   These attempts belonging, to be sure, to other experimental investigations, form counter-attempts, from which we see that the above described characteristic cultures are only to be obtained from substances which contain tuberculous bacilli.

It must still be of special significance for ætiology to determine whether the tuberculous bacilli can grow and multiply under conditions which make possible to them an existence independent from the body of man and of the animals.   For the decision of this question it was first necessary to examine whether the bacilli only grow on the stiffened blood serum or whether they also flourish in other nourishing media.   Attempts with liquid sterilized blood serum gave the result, that little particles of bacilli-culturen, which were put on the surface of the serum in a re-agent glass, developed themselves in the way already described, just as on the surface of the liquid beside the stiffened blood serum, and formed a thin whitish coating, which was of a fragile, brittle consistence, and which broke in moving the serum and sank to the bottom.   The serum always remained clear.   When I did not succeed in keeping the sowed substance floating on the surface of the serum, when it sank into the liquid, the result was no noticeable increase of the sowed pieces.

The blood serum of various sorts of animals showed, as well in a stiffened as in a liquid condition, no essential difference in the power of serving as breeding ground for the tuberculous bacilli.   They appear, to be sure, to flourish best on the serum of sheep, cattle and calves.   But the serum of horse and swine blood gives very vigorous culturen.   Even on the serum of dogs blood the culturen do not grow noticeably less vigorously, in spite of the fact that this species of animals is quite resistent to tuberculosis.   On the contrary, tuberculous bacilli do not grow on the white of eggs.   At first I did not succeed in bringing about the growth of tuberculous bacilli in other liquids than blood serum.   When one or more crumbs of a culture were put into a glass with neutralized meat-broth, the crumbs certainly appeared in the course of four or five weeks to have increased somewhat in size, but it was difficult to decide whether a real growth had taken place.   Not until I had broken the pieces of the bacilli-culture and rubbed them fine, put them into the meat-infusion and by frequent shaking dispersed them through it, that an undeniable development took place.   It does not appear to be unimportant for the success of this attempt, that the culture should be placed in glass alembics with a broad, level base—so-called Erlenmeyer alembics—and only so much liquid put into the alembic as that the bottom be covered from one half to at most the depth of a centimeter. The meat-infusion always remained clear, but in the course of four or five weeks a fine-grained sand-like looking white layer formed at the bottom of the vessel. The single little grains, which had probably grown from the scarcely visible particles of the sowed substance, consisted exclusively of tuberculous bacilli.

If one compares this conduct of the cultures in liquid nourishing media, namely their slow growth and the constant clearness of the liquid, with the reports of former culture attempts from Klebs, Schüller, Toussaint (who noticed after from one to three days a cloudiness of the culture-liquid) one cannot resist the conviction that these cultures could not have been reincultured.

Also in regard to the meat-infusion the phenomenon is repeated, that the flesh of various animals and even of such as are only slightly susceptible to tuberculosis —as dog, cat and domestic mouse—allow the cultures to develop in almost equal strength. It is to be mentioned that neutralized meat-infusion stiffened by an addition of Chinese gelatine, and thereby changed into a firm breeding ground, which can be exposed to the breeding temperature without becoming liquid, also gives a breeding ground for tuberculous bacilli cultures. This is, to be sure, considerably inferior to the stiffened blood serum, because on the slippery surface the bacilli can not be spread out well, and in consequence of this the characteristic membranous cultures are not developed, but instead compact, irregular masses. Since some disease-producing bacteria—for example inflammation-of-the-spleen bacilli, typhus bacilli, glanders bacilli and erysipelas micrococci—grow very vigorously on vegetable substances—for example especially on boiled potatoes—attempts were made in this direction with tuberculous bacilli also, but they have led to no positive results. All in all, therefore, no great scope is offered the tuberculous bacilli in regard to breeding ground.

There are similar limitations with regard to a second condition essential for the existence of bacteria, with the limits of temperature within which growth takes place.

In often repeated attempts it resulted that in a temperature of 42° C. in the course of three weeks no growth took place. Further, in 30° C. the development is very slight and ceases completely between 28° and 29° C. The cultures thrive best in a temperature of 37° to 38° C. A considerably wider range of temperature, within which they can increase, stands at the disposal of other disease-producing bacteria. The inflammation-of-the-spleen bacilli, for example, grow very luxuriantly between 20° and 24° C., and form spores in a short time. They can thrive also up to 43° C. If we take into consideration that the anthrax-bacilli can run the entire course of their development to spore formation in twenty-four to forty-eight hours, in a temperature which in summer is often reached by the surface of the ground, and that they can do this on dead vegetable substrata, the supposition is justified that they can run their course of development in suitable places out of doors and independently of the animal body. No further explanation is necessary to show that, owing to this, the ætiology of anthrax takes an altogether different shape than if the anthrax-bacilli in their existence were dependent alone upon the animal body. The same would hold good of the tuberculous bacilli, if they could grow on breeding substrata such as occur in nature and if they could develop and form spores in a comparatively short time in a temperature corresponding to summer warmth. But this is not the case. The lowest limit of temperature in which the tuberculous bacilli are able to grow is not reached by the summer temperature ; also, the growth of these bacteria goes on so slowly that they would be crowded out by the much more quickly developing sorts of bacteria everywhere appearing before they had finished their course of development. Even if, therefore, other more easily obtainable substrata than those of an animal nature were found, which could serve the tuberculous bacilli as breeding ground, nevertheless the last mentioned reasons would speak decisively against the supposition that the tuberculous bacilli could lead an existence independent of the animal organism. We are, therefore, compelled, so far as our experience reaches, to consider the tuberculous bacilli not as bacilli which can grow anywhere, but as genuine parasites, that is such as can find the conditions of their existence only in the animal or human organism.

D.—ATTEMPTS AT INFECTION.

These attempts until recently have formed the most important part of the experimental investigations concerning tuberculosis. But although these have been carried on in a very extensive manner, they lack, except in a few instances, the prudential measures which must necessarily be united with them to make them free from objection.

There are three sources of error which can raise a doubt in regard to the attempt at infection. First, mistaking spontaneous tuberculosis for the tuberculosis artificially created by infection. Second, the mistaking of products of genuine tuberculous disease for pathological changes, which with the naked eye or even microscopically, more or less resemble them. Third, unintentional infection with tuberculous virus by means of infected instruments, inoculating material, etc., in short through the neglect of antiseptic prudential measures. How shall one protect himself against these sources of error ? To avoid the errors arising from spontaneous tuberculosis, it has been suggested that one experiment only with those animals in which tuberculosis seldom or never occurs. But since animals in which no spontaneous tuberculosis occurs are always more or less indisposed to this disease, and therefore furnish no reliable reagent for the effect of the tuberculous virus, this proposition is practically not feasible. Also for attempts in anthrax infection one would, for example, not chose for exclusive use dogs, which, as is well known, are almost exempt from this disease; but, on the contrary, experiment with animals which are as sensitive as possible to anthrax-infection. The same holds of attempts at infection with tuberculosis. The more sensitive, therefore, a kind of animal is to infection with tuberculous virus, so much the better it is adapted to the infectious attempts in question. Nevertheless only under the condition that one succeeds in keeping the artificial and the spontaneous infection separate in the animals used for experiment. With some little attention this is not so difficult. The characteristic marks by which the two are to be distinguished have already been given in detail. It is self-evident, however, that, even though by means of these characteristics spontaneous tuberculosis be excluded as a cause of mistake, all prudential measures should be taken to confine the spontaneous disease to as narrow a field as possible. This may be attained by separation of the tuberculous animals in different cages, by frequent airing, cleaning and disinfecting of the stalls. Nevertheless it is not advisable permanently to keep rabbits and guinea pigs in the same rooms that contain tuberculous animals; they would scarcely remain free from tuberculosis longer than eight to ten months in infected stalls. In one case a number of animals were kept as long as possible by way of experimenting on their immunity, but in spite of the best care only here and there one remained free from tuberculosis for more than a year, and even these a few months later also became victims to the disease. After all these experiences, all the numerous experiments in which tuberculosis was conclusively shown, have little or no force as proof unless the product itself should make manifest that a spontaneous tuberculosis exists or can be excluded.

As to the second source of mistake, the confusing of non-tuberculous knots with genuine tubercles, nothing is simpler than to exclude the same. The genuine tubercles are infectious and contain tuberculous bacilli; the false do not. Even if one will not admit the diagnostic worth of tuberculous bacilli, one must distinguish between infectious and non-infectious knots. Therefore, if by an attempt at infection, for example if by the inhalation of any substance, some little grey knots be caused in the lung of a dog, one may not content himself with this simple result, and resting upon this claim that these are genuine tubercles. Under all circumstances the infectious nature of such little knots must be proved. Where genuine tuberculosis is concerned one is generally spared the trouble of especially proving their infectious nature by inoculation with the knots, for in this case the disease seldom shows itself confined to one spot; almost always it has already attacked other organs of the body, itself furnishing proof of its infectious nature by its propagating ability. Therefore, when the formation of tubercles stretches itself out past the original infectious spot into the lymph glands, lungs, liver and spleen, it can without further proof be considered infectious. If, as is, for example, the case after the inhalation of non-virulent firm particles into the lungs, and after the injection of granular masses into the "bauchhöhle" (belly cavity) in the peritoneum, the knots caused by this remained confined to the place of infection (here the lungs and peritoneum) and show no inclination to further infection of the body, then this circumstance speaks against the inference that genuine tubercles exist here, and special proof of their infectious nature must be furnished. If this is not done, as it, in an incomprehensible manner, has not been in several of the newer investigations undertaken to prove the non-infectious nature of tuberculosis, then the real proof is lacking in the experiment.

The third mistake mentioned, the unintentional infection by means of instruments, etc., appears to have clung to almost all former investigations with regard to tuberculosis to a greater or less degree, whether such investigations were directed towards proving or disproving its infectious nature. And yet this mistake may be avoided without great difficulty if one holds to the rules concerning antiseptic operations, and above all things carefully disinfects the instrument for every single attempt. All metal instruments, such as scissors, pincers, knives, inoculating lancets, must be heated thoroughly. Special care is demanded in the treatment of the syringes used for injection. Syringes, of ordinary construction cannot be disinfected with sufficient certainty, because they do not admit a high degree of heat without being injured, and liquid means of disinfection, as shown by experience, do not certainly destroy the infectious

material in the interior of the syringe and especially that clinging to the puncturing apparatus.   Hence the syringes must have a special construction which makes
their disinfection by heat possible.   For this purpose the syringe must be made
of glass and metal.   The lower end of the same must be made to have an air-tight
connection with the framework of the needle by means of a cork plate, set
in and bored through; and the piston must be wound with a soft cotton thread.
In this form the syringe can, before every experiment, be made free from infectious germs by an hour's heating at 150° to 160° C.   The piston is then moistened
by absorbing boiled distilled water, and if the enwrapping is done with some care,
it becomes as tight as by the use of the ordinary leather or gutta percha piston.*
The hands of the experimenter are to be disinfected with a one per cent. sublimate
solution, and of course everything else is to be avoided which could lead to an
unintentional infection of the animal to be experimented on during or after the
operation.

By all the attempts at infection to be mentioned in what follows, the prudential measures just explained were strictly carried out and, therefore, to speak again
of the latter, for every attempt several freshly bought animals were used and kept
in separate cages, the effect of the infection was proved so early, that a confusion
with the later appearing spontaneous tuberculosis could not occur; further, the
tuberculous changes appearing in consequence of the infection were always studied
with reference to the presence of tuberculous bacilli, and where it seemed necessary, also especially with reference to their infectious qualities.   The infection
itself took place with antiseptic precaution and especially with reliably disinfected
instruments.

The attempts at infection carried out in the course of my investigations regarding tuberculosis fall into two groups.   To the one group belong those attempts
in which tuberculous bacilli-bearing parts of tissue were used; to the second, those
in which reinculturen of tuberculous bacilli were the infectious material.

E.—ATTEMPTS AT INFECTION WITH TUBERCULOUS BACILLI-BEARING TISSUES.

These served partly for studying the effects of the products of various sorts
of tuberculous processes, partly to gain suitable sowing-material for the beginning
of reinculturen.   As inoculating material there were used pieces of tissue from
various organs of human miliary tuberculosis, from phthisic lungs, various forms
of localized tuberculosis, from fungous joints, scrofulous glands, lupus, tuberculosis
of various animals.   The inoculating material was always examined with reference
to its contents of tuberculous bacilli.   The inoculation took place in this manner:
In guinea pigs a small cut was made with the shears into the belly and by the use
of the points of the shears a pocket-shaped subcutaneous wound about one half
ctm. deep was made in this cut.   Into this little skin pocket a little piece of the
inoculating substance, varying in size from a grain of millet to a mustard-seed,
was pushed in as deeply as possible.   On the following day the inoculation wound
always appeared closed and showed no reaction.   Usually a noticeable swelling
of the lymph-glands lying next to the point of inoculation, usually of the inguinal
glands on one side, first appears after two weeks and at the same time a harden-

*Syringes of this construction are furnished by H. Windler, court instrument maker,
Berlin, N. W. Dorotheenstrasse 3.

ing and knot-forming showed itself upon the up-to-that-time completely healed inoculation-wound. After this the enlargement of the lymph-glands increased rapidly, often to the size of a hazel nut. The knot at the point of inoculation then mostly broke out and covered itself with a dry crust, under which was a flat abscess not discharging much pus and provided with a caseous base. The animals then began to grow emaciated, to have rough hair and difficulty in breathing and died usually from the fourth to the eight week, or were killed within this period. Also in the case of rabbits the inoculating substance was a few times put into a pocket-shaped skin-wound. But since the course of the disease did not run so precisely and so quickly after the subcutaneous inoculation as was the case with guinea pigs, I afterwards chose the anterior eye chamber as the point of inoculation in rabbits. The course of the iris-tuberculosis arising in consequence of this inoculation has been described often and therefore does not need a special description. The following inoculations were carried out in this manner:

1. *Miliary tuberculosis.*—Tuberculous knots of the pia mater, very rich in tuberculous bacilli: six guinea pigs. Of these one died in five weeks, two in six weeks, two in seven weeks after the inoculation. The sixth was killed in the eighth week. In all the animals the lungs, liver and spleen were tuberculous in a high degree and the inguinal glands were caseous.

2. *Miliary tuberculosis.*—Grey little knots of the lung, quite rich in tuberculous bacilli: six guinea pigs. Three died in the sixth week, the others were killed a few days later. All tuberculous as in No. 1.

3. *Miliary tuberculosis.*—Grey yellow knots from the spleen and kidney, not very rich in tuberculous bacilli: six guinea pigs. Died in the sixth and seventh week. All tuberculous as in No. 1.

4. *Miliary tuberculosis.*—Grey knots of the lung, quite rich in bacilli: three guinea pigs. Two died in the sixth, one in the seventh week. All tuberculous as in No. 1.

5. *Miliary tuberculosis.*—Grey knots of the lung containing few bacilli; five guinea pigs, two rabbits at the "root of the ear." One guinea pig died after eight weeks, the others were killed a few days later. All tuberculous. The rabbits killed after ten weeks had caseous lymph-glands at the root of the ear and on the neck, quite a number of grey little knots in the lungs and some knots in the kidneys and in the spleen. Five guinea pigs were inoculated with tubercles from the spleen of one of the guinea pigs. Of these three died in the eighth week, the other two were killed in the same week and all found tuberculous. Further, the caseous gland substance of the rabbits rubbed in water, was injected into the belly cavity of two rabbits. When these animals were killed eight weeks later, tuberculosis of the omentum, spleen and liver existed as also quite a number of grey knots in both lungs.

6. *Caseous pneumonia and tuberculosis of the brain-membranes.*—Two guinea pigs with the bacilli-rich lung-substance, one guinea pig with a piece of the tuberculously infiltrated and bacilli-rich pia mater. The animals died in the fifth and sixth week. Both tuberculous.

7. *Caseously infiltrated lung.*—Six guinea pigs. The first died after six weeks. The others were already very sick and were killed on the following day. All tuberculous.

8. *Phthisic lu..y with vomicæ, intestinal abscesses and caseous mesentric glands.*—With the contents of one vomica, which contained quite a number of bacilli, two guinea pigs were inoculated, and four with the very bacilli-rich substance of the mesentric glands. The last died in the course of the fifth and sixth weeks, of the first two one died in the sixth week, the other was killed a few days later. All tuberculous.

9. *Caseous bronchitis and intestinal tuberculosis.*—With the moderately bacilli-rich lung substance, five guinea pigs were inoculated. Two of them died in the eighth week; the others were killed before the end of the same week. All tuberculous.

10. *A phthisic lung containing vomicæ.*—With thickened lung tissue which contained a few bacilli, four guinea pigs were inoculated. Of these, three died in the seventh and eighth weeks, the last not until the twelfth week. All tuberculous.

11. *Phthisic sputum.* More or less bacilli-rich sputum freshly taken from three different sufferers from phthisis was inoculated at different times into nine guinea pigs. The animals died, part before the eighth week, the others were then killed. They were all tuberculous.

12. *Phthisic sputum dried for two weeks:*—Three guinea pigs. Two died in sixth week, third was then killed. All tuberculous.

13. *Phthisic sputum dried for two months.*—Three guinea pigs. Killed after five weeks and found with tuberculosis in lungs, liver and spleen.

14. *Tuberculosis of the uterus and "tuben."*—Caseous substance from the tuben inoculated into six guinea pigs. Two animals died after seven weeks. The others were killed in nine weeks. All tuberculous.

15. *Pus from a tuberculous abscess of the kidneys.*—Two guinea pigs were sub-cutaneously inoculated with it, and two suffered an injection into the cavity of the belly. The animals were killed after five weeks. In the guinea pigs sub-cutaneously inoculated, the inguinal glands were swollen and beginning to be caseous; in the enlarged spleen were numerous, in the lungs few, little grey knots. The injected guinea pigs had many tuberculous knots on the peritoneum and in the omentum; spleen more strongly tuberculous than in the inoculated animals, a'so larger and more numerous tubercles in the lungs.

16.—*Pus from a congestion-abscess occasioned by aortex-caries.*—Five guinea pigs received from it an injection into the belly cavity. The same boiled distilled water which served for thinning the pus was injected into the belly cavity of one guinea pig which served as co.trol-thier (animal to prove whether association with infected animals would give the disease). This animal was left in the same cage with the others. The animals were killed in the seventh week. The "control-thier" had not a trace of tuberculosis either in the belly cavity or in the lungs. The animals into which the pus was injected showed a remarkably fine tuberculosis of the peritoneum and of the omentum, besides this also a more or less advanced tuberculosis of the spleen and lung.

17.— *Fungous elbow-joint*—Substance with very few bacilli inoculated into four guinea pigs. Killed in the tenth week. All tuberculous.

18.—*Scrofulous glands* from three different cases inoculated into ten guinea pigs at different times. The inoculating substance contained few bacilli and corresponding with this the tuberculosis ran its course much more slowly. Nevertheless also in these animals, the swelling, the first noticeable symptom of disease, and the later caseous degeneration of the inguinal glands, leave no doubt that the place of inoculation formed the point of entrance for the tuberculous virus. Four of the animals died from the tenth to the twelfth week, the others were then killed. In all the lymph glands in the neighborhood of the place of inoculation were caseous, and the spleen, liver and lungs tuberculous to a marked degree.

19.—*Scrofulous gland.*—The gland substance, poor in bacilli, transferred into the anterior eye chamber of four rabbits. In all four animals in the course of the third week, tuberculosis of the iris began to develop and lead to caseous degeneration of the bulbus. In the tenth week the rabbits were killed and beside the destruction of the bulbus, caseous degeneration of the neck lymph-glands and numerous grey knots were found in the lungs.

20.—From five different cases of *lupus* eighteen rabbits were inoculated in the anterior eye-chamber. The course of the disease corresponded exactly with that described in No. 19. An iris-tuberculosis at first developing slowly, gradually leading to caseous degeneration and suppuration of the bulbus and finally to general tuberculosis. The inoculation was without results in the case of one of the rabbits. Some were killed just when the iris-tuberculosis had developed, others after the swelling and caseous degeneration of the neck-glands had appeared; still others finally died with wide-spread tuberculosis of the lung, liver, spleen and kidneys. As well in the tubercles of the iris as in the tuberculously altered glands, lungs, etc., tuberculous bacilli were proved more or less abundantly. From a sixth lupus case three guinea pigs, and from one of the above mentioned cases five guinea pigs were subcutaneously inoculated. In these animals also there were swelling and caseous degeneration of the inguinal glands. They died in the seventh to the eighth week after the inoculation, were tuberculous in a high degree, and had numerous tuberculous bacilli* in the lungs, spleen, liver and kidneys.

21. *Lung affected by "perlsucht"* partially calcareous knots with quite numerous bacilli, inoculated into eight guinea pigs. These died within five to eight weeks and were all tuberculous in a high degree. From one of these guinea pigs four others and from a second three others were inoculated. Of these animals also five died in the sixth and seventh week, the last two were killed in the eighth week. In all these also tuberculosis was found. Further: From the "perlsucht" lung used in these attempts, a cat was inoculated and died after seven weeks, tuberculous. A second cat inoculated with lung tubercles from this animal after six weeks appeared emaciated and short-breathed. She was killed and found to have numerous tubercles in the lungs and spleen.

22.—*A "perlsucht" knot from the peritoneum* inoculated into six guinea

---

*Lately Demme, Pfeifer and Doutrelepont have made communications relating to the occurrence of tuberculous bacilli in lupus-skin and in the tubercles of animals inoculated with lupus. My investigations in regard to lupus, which include not only the proof of bacilli in lupus skin and in inoculation tubercles, but also long continued "rein-culturen" of lupus-bacilli and successful inoculation undertaken with them, had been concluded for several months, when those communications were published, so that these could have had no influence upon my work.

pigs. Three of them died in the fifth and sixth weeks, the others were killed some days later. All tuberculous.

23. *Perlsucht knot from the lung*, partly with caseous contents, and not very rich in bacilli. Seven guinea pigs. Five of them died up to the seventh week. The last two were killed in the eighth week. All tuberculous.

24. *Calcareous perlsucht knot from the peritoneum* with many bacilli. Three guinea pigs; these died up to the sixth week. All tuberculous.

25. *Caseous pneumonia of pig.*—Thickened, very bacilli-rich lung tissue. Five guinea pigs. These died in the fifth and sixth week and were tuberculous.

26. *From the lung tubercles of a rabbit* which died of spontaneous tuberculosis, four guinea pigs were inoculated. Two of these died in the seventh week, two were killed in the eighth week. They were all tuberculous. Four guinea pigs were again inoculated from the first of these animals, two guinea pigs and four rabbits from the second, two rabbits from the third, and one guinea pig and one rabbit from the fourth. The guinea pigs were inoculated subcutaneously, the rabbits in the anterior eye-chamber. The guinea pigs died up to the seventh week of tuberculosis, the rabbits all were attacked with iris-tuberculosis; two died in the ninth and tenth week of tuberculosis, the others were then killed and more or less lung tubercles were found in them.

27. Two guinea pigs and two cats were inoculated with lung tubercles from a monkey, which died of spontaneous tuberculosis. The two guinea pigs died in the sixth week, one cat in the seventh, the other after thirteen weeks. All tuberculous. Six guinea pigs and one rabbit (in the anterior eye-chamber), were then inoculated from one of the guinea pigs and these were all found to be tuberculous before the eighth week (partly died, partly killed). Finally from two animals of this second group the tuberculosis was reinoculated into seven other guinea pigs with success. Also from one of the cats four guinea pigs were successfully inoculated. It is still to be mentioned that four guinea pigs were inoculated with the spleen of this monkey, which had been dried fifty-six days and with the lung tubercles of the same, which had lain fifty-seven days in absolute alcohol. These animals for four months showed no change, were then killed and proved themselves free of tuberculosis.

28. *From a second monkey* which died of spontaneous tuberculosis two guinea pigs were inoculated with lung tubercles and died of tuberculosis in the eighth and ninth weeks. Further: from these guinea pigs two guinea pigs and one rabbit were inoculated. As these appeared already diseased in the sixth week, they were killed and found tuberculous. Two guinea pigs were inoculated with lung tubercles of the same monkey which had been dried and preserved three days. These animals were also killed in the sixth week and found tuberculous.

These experiments in inoculation which have just been enumerated were made upon one hundred and seventy-nine guinea pigs, thirty-five rabbits and four cats, and the inoculation had as a consequence tuberculosis in every case without exception. Moreover the presence of tuberculous changes did not confine itself to single knots of a doubtful nature in one or the other organ, but in every single case the tuberculosis could be proved with all the certainty wished, first, by the development of the characteristic symptoms of the disease, such as swelling of the glands, caseous ulceration of the point of inoculation, emaciation and difficulty of breathing ; second, in dissection by the far advanced and very considerable pathological changes proceeding from the point of inoculation into the neighboring lymph glands and into the lungs, spleen and liver. Moreover, under microscopic examination the characteristic tissue elements of the tubercle and the presence of tuberculous bacilli was always proved. The manner in which the inoculation tuberculosis conducted itself in the different animals and in the different organs has already been described in detail.

Other experimenters have had less favorable results from their inoculations with tuberculous substance. On the other hand the regularly favorable results obtained by me will appear less striking when it is considered that I never used material in which tuberculous bacilli could not be proved, and that for my inoculations I always used those species of animals which are especially disposed to tuberculosis. Besides this, the fact that the inoculations were carried out with all possible care and exactness may have contributed not a little to the results. One might consider it an omission that no attempts were made with the inoculation of non-tuberculous substances. Nevertheless it did not appear to me necessary to make such attempts myself, because, during the course of my investigations, inoculation with the most manifold substances containing no tuberculous bacilli were made by the hundred in the same rooms, and moreover on guinea pigs and rabbits, and a tuberculosis traceable to the inoculation was never found. Especially was non-tuberculous material very often put into the anterior eyechamber and not a single time did tuberculosis of the iris result, while after the inoculation with genuine tuberculous masses it never failed to appear. Besides, the abortive inoculations made with the lung tubercles of the monkey, which tubercles had been dried and preserved in alcohol, described in No. 27, form to a certain extent such attempts, for plainly by the death of the bacilli the tubercles had lost their virulence. The attempt was, therefore, an inoculation with different material.

My attempts, therefore, justify me in the conclusion that only the inoculation with bacilli-bearing substances can cause genuine tuberculosis in the animals used for experiment. A distinction in the effect of inoculation from material coming from tuberculous processes of various kinds, (such as miliary tuberculosis, phthisis, scrofula, fungous diseases of the joints, lupus, perlsucht, and other forms of animal tuberculosis) I have not been able to discover. But also in this regard the various sorts of tuberculosis show a perfectly uniform behavior

F.—EXPERIMENTS IN INFECTION WITH REINCULTUREN OF TUBERCULOUS BACILLI.

This second group of infection experiments forms the conclusion of the proof that tuberculosis is an infectious disease and that it is conditioned upon tuberculous bacilli. Up to this time it has been proved that tuberculous bacilli occur in all tuberculous disease processes and exclusively in these. Further, that only tuberculous bacilli-bearing substances have the power of causing tuberculosis. But since in both cases the bacilli were still united with parts of the body, the supposition was justified that besides the bacilli still another material of importance, perhaps even the real infectious material, might be present while the bacilli played only a secondary part. This question could only be decided by inoculating the bacilli perfectly pure and separate from all parts of the body. If they then also created tuberculosis, they must be the only and indisputable infectious material of tuberculosis. The high importance which belong to just this part of the investigation demanded that the strictest prudential measures should be taken to exclude all errors. With regard to this, as in the former attempts, for every single experiment several freshly bought animals were used. Besides this special counter-acting attempts went along with most of the attempts. The animals of every experiment were in a special cage and were strictly separated from all other tuberculous ones; they were also killed as early as possible to prevent a collision with spontaneous tuberculosis and any objection arising therefrom. Further, as various methods of infection as possible and as various species of animals were used in order to find out the working of the reinculturen in this direction. The greatest care was used in the disinfection of all the vessels and instruments used, especially the syringes. The culturen serving for infection consisted (as was specially proved almost every time), wholly of tuberculous bacilli. The same were lifted with all caution by means of platinum wires heated until red from the stiffened blood serum, which, as has already been expressly mentioned, can easily be done without tearing off the least bit of the blood serum. It is therefore not too much to claim that in most of the attempts absolutely pure bacilli masses were used to which nothing of the breeding ground on which they grew clung. Moreover, in several attempts sterilized blood serum was injected into the animals, which served for the counteracting attempts without the appearance of a trace of tuberculosis. One can therefore claim with all certainty that when genuine tuberculosis is caused by the infection with a tuberculous bacilli-reincultur, which has been continued through several successive breedings, this is to be ascribed alone to the effect of the tuberculous bacilli.

First experiment: Reincultur of miliary tubercles of the human lung (No. 22 in the former enumeration of the reinculturen) cultivated through five successive breedings for fifty-four days, subcutaneously inoculated into four guinea pigs. Two animals in the same cage were not inoculated. In the inoculated animals after forteen days the inguinal glands swelled, the places of inoculation changed into abscesses and the animals began to grow emaciated. One of them died after thirty-two days, the others were killed on the thirty-fifth day. The inoculated guinea pigs, as well the one which died as the three which were killed, showed tuberculosis of the spleen, liver and lungs to a high degree; the inguinal glands were greatly swollen and caseous, and, moreover, decidedly more so on the inoculated side; the bronchial glands were little swelled. The two uninoculated animals showed no trace of tuberculosis.

Second experiment: Reincultur from the tuberculous lung of a monkey, (No. 11) cultivated ninety-five days in eight successive breedings, inoculated subcutaneously into six guinea pigs. Two animals for counter-experiment remained uninoculated. All the animals were killed after thirty-two days and the six inoculated were found tuberculous to a high degree, the two others healthy.

Third experiment: Reincultur from a perlsucht lung (No. 37) cultivated for seventy-two days through six successive breedings, subcutaneously inoculated into five guinea pigs; one animal remained uninoculated. When the animals were killed after thirty-four days the inoculated showed themselves tuberculous, the uninoculated healthy.

Fourth experiment: Reincultur from the tuberculous lung of a monkey (No. 11), cultivated 113 days in nine successive breedings, subcutaneously inoculated into two guinea pigs, one German marmot, six white rats, five white mice, four field mice, two hedge hogs, six domestic fowls, four doves, two sparrows, three eels, one goldfish, five frogs, one turtle. Of these animals only the guinea pigs, the marmot and the field mice became noticeably sick. These were killed fifty-three days after the inoculation and all found tuberculous to a high degree. The tuberculosis of the marmot has, according to all appearance, a very great resemblance to that of the guinea pig. The spleen is very much enlarged and has a greyish-red marbled appearance, also the liver appears permeated by large yellowish herds. The tuberculously changed organs of the field mouse also look very characteristic. The inguinal glands are considerably enlarged and caseous, the lungs permeated by numerous grey knots from the size of a poppy-seed to the head of a pin, and liver and spleen permeated very uniformly with many whitish tubercles as large as a grain of millet, so that these latter gained a very dainty sprinkled appearance. All the other animals of this experiment were killed two months later and it appeared in their investigation, that one of the five white mice had some grey knots in the lungs, the others were healthy, as were also the rats and the hedge hog. Of the domestic fowls, three had the large tuberculous knots in the intestines and in the liver characteristic of this species of animals. The rest of the animals were healthy.

Fifth experiment: Reincultur from the closed vomica of a phthisic lung (No. 26), cultivated for twelve months in sixteen successive breedings and subcutaneously inoculated into seventeen guinea pigs, two other animals remaining uninoculated. With these animals observations were made as to the effect of means which have the power of hindering the development of the tuberculous bacilli and they could therefore not be killed. In spite of the fact that partly arsenic, partly carbolic acid had been used to the greatest possible extent, the tuberculosis ran its course just the same as in the former animals, the lymph-glands swelled considerably, emaciation occurred, all the animals died in the fourth to the sixth week and were tuberculous in a high degree. The two uninoculated animals were then killed and found healthy.

Sixth experiment: The following reinculturen, first, from lupus (No. 35) in eight successive breedings continued for five months; second, from a fungous joint (No. 34) in seven successive breedings for four months; third, from a scrofulous gland (No. 29) in seven successive breedings for five months; fourth, from miliary tuberculosis, (No. 22) in twelve successive breedings for nine months; fifth, from the vomica of a phthisic lung (No. 25) in nine successive breedings for six months; sixth, from a perisucht knot (No. 39) in eleven successive breedings for nine months—were subcutaneously inoculated, and, moreover, from every one of the culturen four animals were inoculated. The mice were put in twos into roomy glasses. Some animals died after a few days, apparently in consequence of the influence of the imprisonment. All the others visibly grew ill, the inguinal glands began to swell, the animals became emaciated and suffered from difficulty of breathing. In the course of four to six weeks they all died. The examination of some of these animals was utterly prevented or only incompletely possible, because the still living field-mice, in spite of having abundant vegetable food, often gnawed their dead comrades and ate up the inner organs of the same with great ravenousness. Nevertheless, from each single division of this experiment some animals remained for examination, and it could therefore be determined that they all perished from a high degree of tuberculosis of the lungs, liver and spleen. A distinction in the conduct of the tuberculosis proceeding from the various reinculturen was not to be recognized. The general appearance of the pathological changes was identical in all animals and so was the appearance of the single little knots to the naked eye, as well as their microscopic conduct and especially their tuberculous bacilli contents. For this experiment it is worthy of notice that the animals had been in imprisonment only a few days when they were inoculated, and that a large number of other field-mice under the same conditions had been kept in glasses for months without a single one of them becoming tuberculous.

Seventh experiment : Since field-mice are such a sure and convenient reagent for tuberculosis, for the purpose of experiments which I made with Dr. Gaffky twenty-four field-mice were subcutaneously inoculated with the reincultur from a phthisic lung (No. 1) cultivated for seven months in twelve successive breedings. These experiments were made in regard to the influence upon tuberculous animals of substances hindering the development. Also from these animals, which were treated with inhalations of easily evaporating substances, some died after a few days of pneumonia, tuberculosis developed itself in all the other, and ran its course in the same way as in the mice of the previous experiment. Under dissection, a well-marked tuberculosis of the lungs, spleen and liver always showed itself.

Eighth experiment : For the same purpose five guinea pigs were inoculated with reincultur from caseous pneumonia (No. 28) cultivated for six months in eight successive breedings; further, four guinea pigs with reincultur from a phthisic lung (No. 24) cultivated for six months in ten successive breedings, and six guinea pigs with reincultur from tuberculosis of the testicles (No. 33) cultivated for three months in five successive breedings—all subcutaneously. These animals had also various gas-like development-hindering substances to breathe in, but in spite of it became sick and emaciated, died within four to six weeks and were under dissection all found tuberculous.

Ninth experiment: Reincultur of lupus (No. 35) cultivated for twelve months in fifteen successive breedings subcutaneously inoculated into five guinea pigs. This experiment was undertaken in order to see whether the continuation of the cultur of tuberculous bacilli from lupus-skin for the space of a whole year had any influence upon the virulence of the same. This was, nevertheless, not the case. The inoculated animals were taken sick just as surely and quickly as in the former experiments; two died in the fourth week, the others were then killed and all found under dissection to be tuberculous in a high degree.

Tenth experiment: With the same intention the longest continued reincultur (No. 1) of human lung phthisis, cultivated for eighteen months in twenty-six successive breedings, was subcutaneously inoculated into four guinea pigs. The course of the disease was just the same as in the ninth experiment. The animals died in the fourth and fifth week of the inoculation and were tuberculous.

Eleventh experiment : By former opportunities an essential difference in the sensitiveness of house mice and field mice to inoculation with tuberculosis had shown itself. Again, therefore, **twelve** white mice were inoculated with a reincultur of miliary tuberculosis (No. 22), the same which **had served in** the inoculation of the field-mice in the sixth experiment, and, moreover, at the same time as the field-mice. While the field-mice, as has already been said, became tuberculous, the white mice remained for two months without any appearance whatever of sickness ; they were then killed and tuberculous changes found in none of them.

These eleven experiments have the one common feature, that the inoculating substance was put into the animals subcutaneously. The effect was in general the same as when fresh tuberculous pieces of tissue were inoculated subcutaneously. The little skin wound closed up and healed in the first days, then followed gland swelling, emaciation, death, and dissection showed a great far-reaching tuberculous erruption in lungs, spleen and liver, with the further characteristic changes of these organs belonging thereto. Only in so far a distinction was noticeable as that after inoculation of the reinculturen the course of tuberculosis was a more rapid one, than after the inoculation of tuberculous tissue. For guinea pigs this difference in time can be reckoned on the average as about two weeks. This appearance explains itself most naturally by the assumption that in the inoculation of tuberculous tissue, the tuberculous bacilli are enclosed by the latter and cannot, therefore, have their effect until the tissue is resorbed, while those in the reinculturen can get immediately into the subcutaneous tissue of the animal, and can immediately begin to act. The same is the case in the inoculation of the anterior eye-chamber of rabbits, and the iris-tuberculosis arising from it, and it is here the case to a more striking degree because the developement of the tubercles can here be observed with the naked eye. Microscopically the tubercles obtained by the inoculation of reinculturen resemble in every way those obtained by the inoculation of genuine tuberculous tissue, and just the same the tubercles arising spontaneously. They consisted of heaps of cells, which mostly had the character of epithelioid cells and closed giant cells, and contained besides the e, tuberculous bacilli in greater or less numbers. Their virulence could be seen from the fact, that in all cases they had spread themselves out from the subcutaneous tissue over all the organs favored by tuberculosis. Besides this, in several cases, farther inoculations were carried out upon other animals and tuberculosis regularly created thereby. The inoculation of the reinculturen remained without effect only in some species of animals, little or not at all sensitive to tuberculosis. On the contrary it made the other numerous animals tuberculous without exception, and as, besides this, all the animals used for counter-experiments remained healthy, there could be no doubt that the question for the decision of which these experiments were undertaken, must be answered in the affirmative, and that the tuberculous bacilli are to be considered the sole cause of tuberculosis.

Nevertheless, it seemed necessary not to stop here, but also to introduce the reinculturen of tuberculous bacilli into animals by all the other methods of infection used up to this time in investigations regarding tuberculosis, in order so to prove in every direction their identity with the tuberculous virus. The methods used up to this time were the following : Inoculation into the anterior eye-chamber of rabbits, injection into the abdominal cavity, injection into one of the larger veins, inhalation of reincultur of tuberculous bacilli.

INOCULATION OF REINCULTUREN IN THE ANTERIOR EYE-CHAMBER.

A cut several millimeters long was made in the cornea, and, moreover, on the upper border of the same, and by means of a blunt hook as small a crumb as possible of a reincultur was pushed through this into the anterior eye-chamber of a rabbit. Some practice and patience are required for this, and on this account I afterward followed another method. The cultur, rubbed to pieces in distilled water, was taken into a syringe, whose needle must be very fine and sharp. The point can easily be pricked through the cornea into the anterior chamber, and the liquid can then be injected into it. This last method is so far more favorable as that the quantity of the infectious material can be very easily controlled. One sees plainly, in moving the piston of the syringe, how the cloudy injecting fluid mingles with the aqueous humor in the eye chamber, and one can inject much or little liquid as he will. A minimum of bacilli can be brought into the anterior chamber, if the needle of the filled syringe be put into it, and without a real injection be taken out again, since traces of the liquid in the needle mix with the water of the chamber, even if the piston of the syringe be not set in motion.

Twelfth experiment : Little crumbs of a reincultur from a caseous-pneumonic lung (No. 27) cultivated for three months in five successive breedings, were put into the anterior eye-chamber of three rabbits. After a few days an intense iritis developed, the cornea soon became cloudy and yellowish gray. The animals then became emaciated very rapidly. They were killed after twenty-five days, and beside the caseous-purulent destruction of the bulbus, swelling and caseous degeneration of the lymph-glands of the lower jaw and of the base of the ear, very numerous tuberculous knots, partly with whitish centres, were found in the lungs.

Thirteenth experiment: Reincultur from a perlsucht lung (No. 19) cultivated for three months in five successive breedings, was rubbed with sterilized blood serum, and injected into the anterior eye-chamber of two rabbits. A third rabbit received just such an injection of pure blood serum. In the case of the first rabbits the same appearances as in the twelfth experiment occurred. Iritis quickly running its course, and cloudiness of the cornea in a few days. The eyes of the third rabbit showed no change. The animals were killed after twenty-eight days. The rabbit into whose eye the pure blood serum had been injected showed itself perfectly healthy ; the other two had caseous bulbi, swollen lymph-glands provided with caseous spots on the lower jaw and beside the base of the ear, and numberless tuberculous knots in the lungs.

Fourteenth experiment : Four rabbits concerned. Pure blood serum was injected into the anterior eye-chamber of the first. The needle of the syringe, which contained blood serum with an addition of reincultur (from tuberculosis of monkey No. 12, cultivated four and one-half months in eight successive breedings) was put into the anterior eye-chamber of the second, but the piston was not moved ; several drops of blood serum mixed with reincultur were injected into the anterior eye-chamber of the third and fourth rabbits. In the case of these last two animals there developed iritis suppuration of the bulbus, followed by rapid emaciation. In the case of the second rabbit, on the contrary, the eye remained unchanged in the beginning and not until the second week did there appear single white yellowish knots on the iris in the neighborhood of the point of injection, and proceeding from this a typical iris tuberculosis developed itself. New little knots constantly appeared on the iris, the iris laid itself into ray-shaped folds, but the cornea gradually became cloudy and thereby hid the other changes from view. The animals were killed after thirty days. The first was perfectly healthy; in the second, aside from the already mentioned changes in the eye, the lymph-glands on the jaw were found swollen and permeated with yellow-white herds, the lungs and other organs were still free from tuberculosis. The two last rabbits had again numberless tubercles in the lungs.

Fifteenth experiment: Reincultur of miliary tubercles from a human lung (No. 4) cultivated for four and one-half months in eight successive breedings, was rubbed up with blood serum and the needle of a syringe filled with it and pricked into the anterior eye chamber of six rabbits without, however, making an injection. In all the animals iris tuberculosis developed, in some of them a slowly spreading infiltration of the conjunctiva with tuberculous knots, reaching beyond the neighborhood of the point of inoculation. Two of the animals of this experiment killed after four weeks had already caseously infiltrated lymph-glands on the neck, but still no tubercles in the lungs. The other rabbits were killed after eight weeks and more or less numerous tubercles were then also found in the lungs.

At various times rabbits received injections of reinculturen in the anterior eye chamber in order to test the influence of substances, which hinder the development of tuberculous bacilli in these animals. Of these attempts which, as has already been mentioned, I carried on with Dr. Gaffky, a report will be given on a later occasion. It may be said here in passing, that beside numerous other means, arsenic, * helenin, sulphuric hydrogen, and moreover always in the largest possible doses and for weeks at a time, were used upon the animals. We cannot state a favorable effect of one of these means in a single case. All the animals perished tuberculously just as quickly as those which had not been treated with means hindering development. The infection took place in various ways; partly by simple inoculation (comp. experiments 7 and 8) partly by injection into the eye-chamber, partly by injection into a vein. The rabbits infected from the eye-chamber concern the following cases:

Sixteenth experiment: Reincultur of miliary tubercles of the human lung (No. 22) cultivated for eight months in ten successive breedings, rubbed up with distilled water and injected into the anterior eye chamber of two rabbits; Reincultur from a phthisic lung (No. 1) cultivated for thirteen months in twenty-one successive breedings, injected in the same way into fifteen rabbits. Some of the same reincultur one month later injected into six rabbits. All these rabbits perished

---

* The use of arsenic to fight tuberculosis has been often recommended in former times and tried by many physicians. It was therefore natural to test the influence of this on tuberculous animals. Our experiments occurred almost a year before the recommendation of arsenic by Buchner appeared, and were, therefore, not induced by that. According to Korab, helenin has prevented tuberculosis and sulphuric hydrogen was warmly recommended by Froschauer.

quickly with the already described symptoms and had always numerous tuberculous knots in the lungs.

In all the cases of these experiments, in which very small quantities of the
reincultur were successfully brought into the anterior eye-chamber, the effect was
exactly the same as after the inplantation of the natural tuberculous virus in the
anterior eye-chamber. Single tuberculous knots appeared in the iris, which increased in number and led to caseous degeneration of the bulbus and finally to
general tuberculosis. In so far, to be sure, a distinction existed in that the eruption of little knots occurred earlier than after the inoculation with tuberculous
tissue. The probable ground of this appearance has already been discussed. A
very noteworthy fact has been gained from the experiments, namely, the considerable difference in the effect according as a small number of bacilli or a large
quantity of the same get into the eye-chamber. In the first case we see a process
slowly creeping on, in which the infectious material first spreads itself upon the
iris, then reaches the lymph-glands, makes these caseous and not until then forcing
itself into the course of the blood and so becoming sowed over other organs of the
body. If, on the contrary, a large number of bacilli are in the beginning deposited
in the anterior eye-chamber, then it has an appearance suggesting that the before-
mentioned way is unnecessary. Especially it appears as if the lymph-glands,
which usually offer an opposition to the progress of the bacilli and hold them
fast for a longer or shorter time, were passed over altogether. The appearance of
very numerous tuberculous knots in the lungs, spleen, etc., occurs as early in this
mode of infection as after the injection of tuberculous bacilli immediately into a
vein. Also the quantity of the little knots after the injection into the anterior eye-
chamber does not compare very unfavorably with the quantity of them after injection into the course of the blood. Now whether the explanation of this is to be
sought therein, that the bacilli of the anterior eye-chamber can really in any way
come direct into the course of the blood in quantities, or whether their great number, which suddenly overflows the lymph passages and glands lying before us,
causes most of the bacilli to break through the hindrance, so that only a few remain, that I must leave undecided. At all events this appearance is adapted to
give enlightenment as to the apparently inexplicable irregular conduct of tuberculosis with reference to the duration of its course and to the longer or shorter
local confinement.

INJECTION OF REINCULTUREN INTO THE ABDOMINAL CAVITY.

The reinculturen, rubbed up with blood serum or distilled water, were filled
into a disinfected syringe, the point of operation on the abdomen of the animal
was disinfected with sublimate solution, and then the needle slowly driven through
the covering of the abdomen so that the intestines remained unhurt, and then the
liquid was squirted into the abdominal cavity. This of itself very simple operation can easily be performed upon animals whose intestines are not constantly
filled with firm, unyielding matter, and I have always succeeded with guinea pigs,
rats, mice, cats, etc., without causing injury to the intestines or traumatic perito-
nitis. Rabbits are less adapted for this experiment on account of the closely filled
coecum. In order to obtain as quick an effect as possible, considerable masses
of reincultur were always injected. The abdominal cavity, like the eye-chamber,

reacts differently according to the different quantities of tuberculous virus. After an injection of pus containing few bacilli there arose on the peritoneum, as we have already seen, a disseminated tuberculous eruption, then a development of little knots in the omentum and the spleen. But when masses of tuberculous bacilli were injected into the abdominal cavity of guinea pigs, then they were principally taken up by the large omentum. This rolls itself together and forms a horizontally-extending, thick, sausage-like roll, which on intersection has the greatest resemblance to an intersected, greatly swollen, and freshly caseous lymph-gland. In these white-yellowish, quite compact herds of the omentum enormous quantities of tuberculous bacilli are found, most of which are in a fine state of spore formation. Besides this, as microscopic investigation shows us, the swollen spleen, the liver and the peritoneum are abundantly supplied with tuberculous bacilli, but the death of these animals occurs so early that the development of knots visible to the naked eye has not had time to occur. An effusion of liquid was not found in the abdominal cavity of guinea pigs, but was found in dogs and cats. On the contrary, in guinea pigs, such a large quantity of clear, faintly yellow liquid was found in the pleura that the lungs were compressed by it, and this caused the death of the animal. The guinea pigs usually died ten to twenty days after the injection. If a smaller quantity of culture substance is squirted in, the course of the disease is of longer duration and there is then a development of visible, extraordinarily numerous tuberculous knots, particularly upon the peritoneum, on omentum, in the spleen and liver. The species of animals less subject to tuberculosis—dogs, rats, white mice—do not succumb even to the injection of abundant bacilli until after some months. But they then show also an unusually abundant tuberculous eruption in the abdominal organs, but, on the contrary, less numerous knots in the lungs.

Seventeenth Experiment : Reincultur from the tuberculous lung of a monkey (No. 11) cultivated for six months in eleven successive breedings, was rubbed up with blood serum and injected into ten guinea pigs, a half cubic centimeter into each. Two animals for counter experiment received, the one just such an injection of pure blood serum, the other, which had a fresh, large wound from a bite, no injection at all. Of the animals which had received the injection, deaths occurred after ten, thirteen, sixteen, seventeen, eighteen days. The others, as well as the "controlthiere*" were killed on the twenty-fifth day. In the guinea pig which died first the large omentum was rolled together, greatly thickened, and infiltrated with a yellowish-white brittle substance ; no knots were visible on the liver and spleen. The other animals of this experiment, as well those which died as those which were killed, had, besides infiltration of the omentum, already tuberculous eruption of the spleen and liver. The controlthiere were perfectly healthy.

Eighteenth Experiment : Reincultur of the tuberculous lung of a monkey (No. 11) cultivated for five and one-half months in ten successive breedings, rubbed up with blood serum, was injected into the abdominal cavity of two full grown vigorous cats. The one cat died after nineteen days. The omentum was rolled together, very much thickened, and infiltrated with a whitish compact mass. The serous covering of the intestines and the peritoneum had lost its lustre, the

* Animals for counter experiment.

spleen was greatly enlarged. The infiltration of the omentum consisted, as in the guinea pigs of the previous experiment, of thick masses of tuberculous bacilli, embedded mostly in cells. With the naked eye no knots could be seen in the lungs, spleen and liver, but microscopically these organs were permeated already by an unusually abundant tuberculous eruption. The second cat was killed after forty-three days, and there were already tuberculous knots as large as a millet seed in great numbers, quite uniformly spread over the lungs, spleen and omentum, while in the liver the number was comparatively small. Both cats were to have received a syringefull of the injecting liquid, therefore an equal quantity, but the second was very uneasy during the operation and only a small part of the liquid could be successfully injected ; on which account the tuberculosis had a considerably longer course, and fewer tuberculous knots developed which had time to reach a considerable size.

Nineteenth Experiment: Reincultur of miliary tuberculosis (No. 22) cultivated for three months in five successive breedings, rubbed up with blood serum, and two cubic centimeters of this liquid injected into the abdominal cavity of a female dog several years old. A half cubic centimeter of the same liquid was injected into a male dog some months old. In the first weeks after the injection no change could be seen in the animals. After the third week the female dog lost her briskness, she ate less, and a noticeable swelling of the body occurred. This animal was killed at the beginning of the fifth week. In the abdominal cavity was a quite abundant effusion of a clear, faintly yellowish liquid. The omentum, mesenterium, ligaments of the womb and peritoneum were sprinkled over with many tuberculous knots, as were also the surface of the intestines and bladder. The enlarged spleen, the liver and lungs contained numerous miliary tubercles provided with tuberculous bacilli. The places of injection could no longer be recognized. The second dog appeared sick for a time, had also plainly an effusion of liquid in the abdominal cavity, and became emaciated ; finally it recovered and developed very vigorously. This dog, together with a female from the same litter, received five months later an injection from the same reincultur, this time however of two cubic centimeters. The result was the same in both animals : for some weeks they showed no symptoms of disease, then became emaciated and were attacked by ascites. One animal died after five weeks, and then the other, which was already very weak, was killed. The information gained from the dissection was exactly the same as in the case of the first dog. Omentum, peritoneum, spleen, liver and lungs were supplied with extraordinarily many tuberculous knots.

This experiment is in so far of special interest as that one dog after the injection of a half cubic centimeter of bacilli liquid was, to be sure, taken sick, but recovered. This is the only case of tuberculosis in animals which I have seen recover. The hope has often been expressed that, as in the case of inflammation of the spleen, a preventive inoculation with weakened virus might be used against tuberculosis. But if one recovery from tuberculosis gives protection against a second attack of the disease, for which, by the way, experience by the sick bed gives no ground of hope, then this dog should have had immunity against further experiments in infection. But this was not the case, and this circumstance speaks against the justification of such hopes.

Twentieth experiment : Of five cats the first received an injection of pure blood serum, died; second the same serum with an addition of reincultur No. 23 (miliary tubercles of man, cultivated for five months in eight successive breedings;) the third from reincultur No. 1 (lung phthisis of man, cultivated for seven months in twelve successive breeds); the fourth from reincultur No. 16 (perlsucht knot, cultivated for five and a half months in nine successive breedings); the fifth from reincultur No. 13 (tuberculosis of monkey cultivated for three months in five successive breedings). Just the same was done with five guinea pigs. Of the last, one each died on the twelfth, fourteenth, fifteenth and twenty-first days. The controlthier was killed on the twenty-second day. Of the cats the fourth died on the twenty-second day, the third on the twenty-seventh day, the other animals were killed on the twenty-eighth day. All the animals into which the bacilli liquid had been injected showed the familiar tuberculous changes in a state of development corresponding with the space of time since the injection. As well the cat as the guinea pig into whose abdominal cavities pure blood serum had been injected, were wholly free of tuberculosis. This experiment, like several previous ones, was undertaken to test any possible differences which might exist in the results of bacilli culturen originating in the various forms of tuberculosis. But this time also the expectation cherished was not fulfilled; for the tuberculosis generated by the various reinculturen conducted itself exactly the same in all, in the cats as well as in the guinea pigs.

Twenty-first experiment: Reincultur from tuberculosis of monkey (No. 11, cultivated for five months in ten successive breedings) was injected into the abdominal cavity of five rats. These animals were fed for some time beforehand with the dead bodies of tuberculous guinea pigs. In the case of other rats which belonged to the same feeding experiment and had been killed, only individual grey knots had been found a few times. But when the rats, into whose abdominal cavity tuberculous bacilli had been injected, were killed, after five weeks, numberless tuberculous knots were found in the lungs, in the greatly enlarged spleen, and in the liver and omentum.

Twenty-second experiment: Reincultur (No. 24, from a phthisic lung, cultivated for five months in nine successive breedings), rubbed up in distilled water, was injected into the abdominal cavity of the following animals; six guinea pigs, three cats, four white mice, four domestic fowls, eight doves. The guinea pigs died in from ten to seventeen days, the cats one each on the fifteenth, twenty-third and twenty-fourth days. The results as found in the dissection were the same as in the other experiments. The mice, fowls and doves, to be sure, remained alive, but were rough, thin, and seemed sick. As they did not recover, they were all killed at the end of ten weeks. The mice showed the same appearance as the white rats; they had quite numerous tuberculous knots in the lungs and very many in the greatly enlarged spleen. In the fowls and doves were found such knots as have already been described in the intestines and in the liver.

INJECTION OF REINCULTUREN IN THE VEINS.

By this method the infection of the animal is wrought most quickly and in the manner most productive of result. The body is at once overflowed by means of the blood with as great a quantity of the infectious matter as one wishes. Said matter has no need to overcome the hindrances put in its way, by the lymph-glands, etc., as when other methods are used, but spreads itself immediately over all the organs and causes a great and quite uniformly distributed tuberculous eruption. The mode of infection has plainly the greatest resemblance to that of miliary tuberculosis in man, where the tuberculous virus also makes its way into the blood and so is carried everywhere. By the help of injection into the veins tuberculous knots can be called forth in all the organs in such short time, and in so enormous numbers as is never the case in spontaneous tuberculosis; a mistaking of one for the other is therefore here completely excluded. The liquid in which the reinculturen of tuberculous bacilli were divided as finely as possible was filtered through fine gauze, in order to keep back all coarser particles, and then injected with one of the formerly described disinfected syringes, into the vena jugularis, or according to Aufrecht's example, direct into the ear-vein of a rabbit which had been laid bare.

Twenty-third experiment : Of twelve rabbits, two had a half cubic centimeter of pure blood serum injected into the ear-vein ; four rabbits received in the same manner blood serum with an addition of reinculter No. 11 (tuberculosis of monkey, cultivated for six months in eleven successive breedings—compare the seventeenth experiment) ; three rabbits blood serum with reinculter No. 1 (from phthisic lung cultivated for six months in ten successive breedings); three rabbits, blood serum with reinculter No. 19 (perlsucht lung, cultivated four months in seven successive breedings). In the first days after the operation nothing striking was to be noticed in any of these rabbits. The two first remained brisk and vigorous, all the others began to breathe hard in the second week, and became emaciated with unusual rapidity. The first rabbit (injection with cultur No. 1) died after eighteen days ; the second and third (injection with cultur No. 11) after nineteen days ; the fourth (cultur No. 19) after twenty-one days ; the fifth (cultur No. 1) after twenty-five days ; the sixth and seventh (cultur No. 11) after twenty-six and twenty-seven days ; two other animals on the thirtieth and thirty-first days. The last and the two controlthiere were killed on the thirty-eighth day after the injection. In the conduct of the lungs and other organs of the animals treated with the various culturen, as in former similar experiments, no distinction could be observed. In all the animals numberless miliary tubercles were found in the lungs. The liver and spleen of all these animals contained an extraordinary number of tubercles. In those which died first the knots were smallest, but also most numerous. It was plain that the great number of tubercles had caused such an early death. In the animals dying later the number of knots was somewhat smaller, but their size, on the contrary, decidedly larger. The two controlthiere were found on dissection without a deposit of tubercles in any organ.

Twenty-fourth experiment : Pure culture of lupus, No. 35 (cultivated for five months in eight successive breedings), rubbed up with distilled water and injected into the ear-veins of five rabbits. These died from the thirteenth to the eighteenth day after the injection and in the dissection showed the same state of things as in the rabbits of the former experiment.

Twenty-fifth experiment : Pure culture of monkey tuberculosis No. 11 (cultivated for six months in twelve successive breedings), rubbed up with distilled water, was injected into the vena jugularis of ten rabbits which were intended for experiments in inhalation with means of hindering the development. They all died in the course of two to three weeks after the injection and had great quantities of tubercles in lungs, liver and spleen.

The tuberculous knots generated by injection into the course of the blood, like all the other infections brought about by pure cultures, were not to be distinguished from the tubercles arising spontaneously. They contained tuberculous bacilli in greater or lesser numbers and were virulent, for, when inoculated into other animals, as was frequently done, they caused tuberculosis in the same manner as the inoculations with genuine, spontaneous tuberculosis.

INHALATION OF PURE CULTURES OF TUBERCULOUS BACILLI.

In order to bring tuberculous substances into the lungs of animals to be experimented on, either from a tracheotomic wound an injection was made into the bronchiæ, or the infectious mass suspended in a liquid was made into spray and breathed in by the animals. The first method does not sufficiently correspond with the natural mode of infection, and is complicated in a disturbing manner by the wound necessary for the operation. On that account I have chosen the second method, which to be sure, for evident reasons, is not without danger to the experimenter, and hence demands especial precautions.

The experiment was carried out in the following way: a very roomy box with an opening on one side for the mouth of the atomizing apparatus, was placed in a garden at a sufficient distance from inhabited rooms. The atomizing apparatus was put on the outside of the box and projected with its mouth into the interior of the box. By means of a rubber and a suitably long lead pipe which was put through the wooden framework of a closed window, the apparatus was connected with the rubber bellows, and could so be set in motion from the room without the necessity of the experimenter's venturing within reach of the atomized liquid.

Twenty-sixth experiment: Pure culture from a human phthisic lung (No. 1) cultivated fifteen months in twenty-three successive breedings was rubbed up with distilled water and the liquid so thinned that it appeared almost clear. What visible crumbs were still present in the liquid were deposited after a short rest, and the upper layers of the liquid, showing scarcely any cloudiness, were poured off and used for inhalation. On three successive days, each time in the course of half an hour 50 cctm. were atomized and inhaled by the following animals in the box: eight rabbits, ten guinea pigs, four rats, four mice. After the inhalation the animals were kept in separate cages, and well taken care of. In some animals, in ten days difficulty of breathing showed itself; then three rabbits and four guinea pigs died in from fourteen to twenty-five days. All the other animals were killed twenty-eight days after the last inhalation. All the rabbits and guinea pigs had numerous tubercles in the lungs, varying in size according to the length of time the animal had lived after the inhalation. In the animals dying latest, in those killed there were already tubercles in the liver and spleen. The tubercles in the lungs were in every respect exactly like those which were obtained in guinea pigs and rabbits through inhalation of phthisic sputum in experiments undertaken for other purposes. Especially the tuberculous knots generated by inhalation of phthisic sputum and those generated by the inhalation of pure cultures had that in common, that when they had reached a certain size their alveolar spreading could already be plainly recognized by the naked eye. They did not appear sharply rounded off and circumscribed, but embraced mostly the centre of a lobulus. As the single alveoli were filled with a caseous mass and hence appeared as fine whitish little points, they had a dull fine-grained appearance, and on their border the white-yellowish little points of the caseous alveoli showed themselves very plainly against the dark, greyish-red circle. The largest tuberculous knots embraced an entire lobulus and sometimes ran together into neighboring knots, in this manner forming larger, thickened, white-yellowish places in the lung which repeated completely the appearance of caseous pneumonia. The spontaneous tuberculosis occurring in rabbits and guinea pigs also shows in the structure of the primary tuberculous knots the conduct just described, namely, the alveolar spreading of the tuberculous process. This circumstance, therefore, confirms the view already expressed, that the spontaneous tuberculosis of these animals is almost exclusively an inhalation tuberculosis.

The rats and mice which were killed had very numerous little grey knots to the size of a hemp seed in the lungs, many of which possessed a white-yellowish centre, yet the caseous degeneration was by far not so advanced as in the lungs of the guinea pigs and rabbits. In the spleen of the rats and mice also, only single grey knots were found. These animals, as has already been often made prominent, are far less sensitive to tuberculosis, the single tubercles develop in them much more slowly, and the further spread of the tuberculosis to other organs does not occur so easily.

Also microscopically the tubercles arising from inhalation of pure cultures resemble completely the genuine tubercles in the arrangement of the epithelioid cells, the giant cells, and the contents in tuberculous bacilli. In order to prove the infectious properties of the same, twenty-two guinea pigs were inoculated subcutaneously in the abdomen with tubercles from various organs, as well from several guinea pigs as from rabbits and from the lung of a rat and of a mouse. These without exception were very soon attacked by swelling of the inguinal glands on the side of the inoculation, became emaciated and died in course of five to eight weeks of tuberculosis.

If we look over all the experiments with pure cultures we reach the following results:

Those animals which belong to species easily susceptible to tuberculosis, namely, guinea pigs, rabbits, field-mice and cats, became tuberculous without exception in consequence of the infection with tuberculous bacilli. The number of these animals amounts to two hundred and seventeen (ninety-four guinea pigs, seventy rabbits, nine cats and forty-four field mice). A number of animals for counter experiments, treated in like manner with indifferent liquids, and kept under the same conditions, on the contrary, without exception, remained free from tuberculosis. Of the less susceptible animals, as a result of a simple subcutaneous inoculation, only domestic fowls, and, moreover, only half of those inoculated, became tuberculous. But even dogs, rats and white mice, which are usually very slightly susceptible to tuberculosis, could not withstand the infection with large quantities of purely cultivated tuberculous bacilli, and also without exception, became tuberculous.

The various methods of infection used had the same effect with the pure cultures as with the natural tuberculous substances, only the first had a some-what quicker effect than the last.

The products of the infection also were exactly like those obtained with the natural infectious material, as well in their microscopic structure as in their contents of tuberculous bacilli and in their virulent properties.

By the most careful attention to all the prudential measures needful for the avoidance of mistakes in experimenting with tuberculosis, errors are with certainty excluded from these experiments. With reference to this it may also be made prominent here that in the same manner as with tuberculous bacilli, an extraordinary number of experiments with other disease-producing and non-disease-producing bacteria were made. These were also put into the anterior eye-chamber of rabbits, or were injected into their veins, they were subcutaneously inoculated into rabbits, guinea pigs, mice, etc., and injected into the abdominal cavity. Other bacteria were also used for experiments in inhalation according to the method already described. But tuberculosis was never generated in these animals by these means.

In these experiments made with pure cultures, also only the tuberculous bacilli completely freed from all original products of the disease, can have been the cause of the tuberculosis. The proof of the proposition that tuberculosis is an infectious disease conditioned upon tuberculous bacilli, is herewith concluded. One could be sure to say, and it has been said, that the tuberculous bacilli are one cause for the occurrence of tuberculosis, but that besides these other things, for example other micro-parasites, can likewise generate tuberculosis. This supposition is, nevertheless, erroneous, because as we have seen, in all cases of genuine tuberculosis, tuberculous bacilli occur, and the manner of their occurrence allows us to infer a causative connection with the disease. If in spite of this one would claim that besides the tuberculous bacilli still another special tuberculous virus exist, that would justify a claim that beside trichinæ and itch-mites still another specific, until now unknown agent must exist as infectious material. We can, therefore, with right say that the tuberculous bacilli are not only one cause, but the only cause of tuberculosis, and that without tuberculous bacilli there is no tuberculosis.

Therewith, tuberculosis is joined to inflammation of the spleen in knowledge of its ætiology. The tuberculous bacilli stand in just the same relation to tuberculosis as the inflammation of the spleen bacilli to that disease.

G.—THE RELATIONS OF THE TUBERCULOUS BACILLI TO THE ÆTIOLOGY OF TUBERCULOSIS.

The investigations communicated in the preceding have already gained us so much knowledge of the biologic properties of the tuberculous bacilli, and their peculiar behavior in the body attacked by them, that by their help the ætiology of tuberculosis in its outlines may be stated with certainty. In time we shall certainly become more thoroughly acquainted with the properties of tuberculous bacilli, and find out much that is new about them, which will extend our views of the ætiology of tuberculosis, and in many ways amend them; nevertheless, this conviction cannot prevent us from forming an opinion now as to the relations of tuberculous bacilli to the disease caused by them.

If we start from the experimentally proved proposition that only tuberculous bacilli have the power of generating genuine tuberculosis, and if we apply ourselves to following the way which the bacilli take in the infection, the question of the origin of the bacilli first forces itself upon us. Do they occur anywhere, and independent of the human or animal organism, in the outer world, as for example must be concluded of the inflammation of the spleen bacilli and the micrococci of erysipelas? The answer to this question is of the greatest importance, not only for the ætiology, but also much more for the prophylaxis. For, granted the tuberculous bacilli live in the decaying animal or vegetable materials everywhere to be found, that they can increase and form spores, then it would hardly be possible to keep these parasites away from man. But fortunately it is otherwise. Experience has taught that the tuberculous bacilli grow much more slowly than all other bacteria ; further, that they only grow in blood serum and meat liquid, and, which is the main point, they need temperatures of more than 30° C. in order to thrive. Also, when all these conditions were found united, but the tuberculous bacilli were not protected against the luxuriant growth of other quickly growing bacteria, then, as one can often enough see in the cultures corrupted by foreign bacteria, the bacilli would be crowded out and killed by the rival bacteria. Now, indeed, the conditions of development favorable for tuberculous bacilli, especially the warmth of 30° C. day and night for weeks are found united nowhere except in the animal organism, and there is, therefore, no other supposition possible than that they are dependent for their existence wholly upon the animal and human organisms. They are therefore, genuine parasites, which cannot exist without a body to support them. They are not like the anthrax-bacilli, accidental parasites, which usually complete their course of development in the outer world and only occasionally make an invasion into the animal body. There exists also an essential difference between the anthrax-bacilli and the tuberculous bacilli, in that the first only multiply in the animal body, but never form spores, and for the development into the permanent form must get into the outer world again, while the tuberculous bacilli complete their entire course of development in the body and in no way need a life in the outer world in order to take the form necessary for the preservation of the species.

Another question is, whether from the wide-spread bacteria, which often get into the body, under favorable conditions, by means of adaptation and successive breedings, tuberculous bacilli might not arise, or on the other hand the tuberculous bacilli either in the body or after they had left the same might not change into harmless bacteria. It would then not need the invasion of specific bacteria to develop tuberculosis, but all would depend on the necessary preparatory conditions for changing harmless into harmful bacteria, which would be all the same as one usually calls tendency. The representation of a cross-breeding of tuberculous bacilli corresponds exactly with the now often held but widely exaggerated views of the changeable nature of bacteria, and has already found supporters. More value than that of a purely hypothetical view it can, nevertheless, not claim, **for no facts speak for it, but many against it.** A certainly proved example of **a breeding of harmful bacteria from** harmless ones, as is **well** known, does **not yet exist, and there is,** therefore, no ground for ascribing to tuberculous bacilli **origination of that sort from** indifferent bacteria. **There is so** much the less **reason for this, since among the** numberless **experiments in** animals with **disease-producing and non-disease-producing bacteria, it has never occurred that in the so very favorable breeding ground of the bodies of rabbits and guinea pigs,** tuberculous bacilli have developed from other bacteria. **On the contrary, all** experiments undertaken with the necessary precautionary **measures teach** that tuberculosis only arises when genuine, that is to **say, complete tuberculous bacilli are** united with the animal body.

The relations are different in regard to an eventual weakening of the tuberculous bacilli, since the weakening of the anthrax-bacilli can be cited for the possibility of such a proceeding. Although the possibility of such a change in the virulence is not to be disputed, nevertheless it must be considered that the weakening of the anthrax-bacilli is completed under circumstances which can only be brought about artificially, but which do not come into play in ordinary circumstances either in the body or out of it. Moreover, against such a supposition the fact speaks, that tuberculous bacilli do not show the slightest change in their qualities, especially in their virulence, when successive breedings have been carried on in cultures, that is to say out of the animal body, and on a dead breeding substratum almost two years. Also in the experiments of Fischer and Schill, which are reported in another part of this paper, when tuberculous bacilli had been exposed for six weeks to the influence of decay, no weakening of the virulence occurred. All this speaks with decision against the supposition of an easily occurring change in the virulent properties of the tuberculous bacilli. It is, perhaps, inconceivable that the bacilli did not at some time proceed from other bacteria. But after they had once become genuine parasites, they appeared to have the peculiarity common to other parasites of holding to their qualities with great obstinacy.

The only source for the origin remains, therefore, the animal or human organism, and opportunity is not lacking to these parasites, owing to the extraordinary diffusion of tuberculosis, to reproduce themselves in this field in enormous masses, to develop the permanent form, to get into the outer world, and to attack other victims.

Among the various forms of tuberculosis there are, to be sure, only certain ones which admit an easy transference of the bacilli. But these are exactly the most frequently occurring forms, namely, phthisis and the tuberculous diseases of the domestic animals. The other sorts of tuberculosis play almost no part in reference to infection, partly because they remain so hidden that they can only exceptionally cause infection.

If we ask first in how far phthisis can cause a transference of tuberculous bacilli from diseased to healthy people, it is quite evident that here all the conditions for the spread of the infectious material are present in fullest measure. One only needs to remind himself that on the average one-seventh of all men die of phthisis, and that most phthisic patients, at least for some weeks, often for months, throw out great quantities of sputum in which enormous quantities of spore-bearing tuberculous bacilli are contained. Of these numberless infectious germs, which are spread everywhere on the ground, on articles of clothing, etc., much the greater part perish again, without ever finding opportunity to establish themselves anew in a living organism. If one farther considers, that according to the experiments of Fischer and Schill already mentioned, the tuberculous bacilli can retain their virulence in a decaying sputum for forty-three days, and in dry air sputum for one hundred and eighty-six days, then with regard to the great number of tuberculous bacilli produced by the phthisically diseased, and to the endurance of the bacilli in a damp as well as dry condition, it is easy to see and explain the enormous diffusion of the tuberculous virus.

As to the method in which tuberculous virus is transmitted from the diseased to the healthy no doubt can obtain. In consequence of shocks from coughing of the diseased person, little particles are rent from the tough sputum, sent into the air and so dispersed like dust. Now numerous experiments have taught that the inhalation of finely dispersed phthisic sputum not only makes those sorts of animals sensitive to tuberculosis, but also those capable of resistance tuberculous with absolute certainty. That man should be an exception to this is not to be supposed. It may, therefore, be taken for granted that when a healthy human being accidentally finds himself in the immediate neighborhood of the phthisically diseased, and inhales particles of sputum sent forth into the air, he can be infected by them But infection taking place in this manner will probably not occur very often, because the bits of sputum are usually not so small that they can long remain suspended in the air. Far more adapted for infection is, on the contrary, the dried sputum, which, owing to the careless way in which the sputum of consumptives is treated, can plainly get into the air in considerable quantities. Not only is the sputum spit directly upon the ground, there dried and trodden under foot and stirred up in the form of dust, but it often becomes dried and made into dust from the bed clothes, articles of clothing and especially from handkerchiefs, which are soiled even by the most cleanly patients by wiping the mouth after expectorating the dangerous infectious material. The experiences which have been gained from the investigation of the air, with reference to bacteria capable of development, have taught that the bacteria are not suspended in the air in an isolated condition, but that they, with the liquids in which they have grown, dry on the surface of objects and only get into the air when the dried up mass breaks off in little bits, or when the bearers of the dry bacteria liquid themselves are so light that they can be carried away by the lightest breath of air. As such easily moved bearers, little bits of dust act best, which consist of fragments of plant fibres, animal hair, epidermis scales and similar materials. On that account defilement from vegetable tissues and animal hairs and bed clothes, clothing and handkerchiefs, when caused by phthisic sputum are most to be feared. From spittoons and from the floor dried sputum can only be separated in larger particles, which are not easily raised up into the air; on the contrary, one can scarcely conceive a more favorable arrangement for the dispersion of the sputum particles than the rapid drying on cloth, from which with every motion little threads separate themselves, which carry the infectious material into the air, remain suspended comparatively long, and when they finally sink to the ground are whirled up again by the lightest breath of air. The investigations of the air carried on by Hesse are specially instructive on this subject.

As has already been mentioned, the virulence of the dried sputum can be preserved for months; under some circumstances perhaps longer. The last qualities of the virulence depend probably upon its containing well developed spores capable of developing germs. In any case, even if the dried sputum retains its virulence only a few weeks, a consumptive in the condition in which one generally finds these sick persons is very well adapted to provide his immediate surroundings with abundant quantities of infectious material, and, moreover, in the most favorable form for the causing of infection.

When the tuberculous bacilli are inhaled in dust-form, then they can either remain in the upper air passages or force themselves into the alveoli just as is the case with other inhaled particles of dust. The depth to which they enter the respiratory tract will depend essentially on the manner of breathing; if breathed deep and with open mouth, they will get in farthest. Breathing through the nose will, on the contrary, guaranty a certain protection against the entrance of the bearers of the infectious material, since a considerable quantity of dust of the air breathed is retained by the mucous membrane of the nose. But whether the tuberculous bacilli, when they reach the bronchii and alveoli, are able to take firm hold and establish themselves will depend on many circumstances. Especial influence on this will be exercised by the slow growth of the tuberculous bacilli. Other disease-producing bacteria, for example the anthrax bacteria, appear in consequence of their rapid growth to grow very soon to such an extent and to exercise so quickly a harmful influence on the cells in their neighborhood, that the ciliated epithelium of the mucous membrane of respiration is no longer able to master and dispose of them; they can on that account establish themselves in the upper sections of the respiratory passages and call forth the pathological processes peculiar to them. This is taught by the wool sorters' disease and especially the affection running its course under the term of anthrax of the larynx. Quite different are the relations for tuberculous bacilli. These need as many days as the anthrax bacilli hours to reach a development worth mentioning, and before they reach it are in ordinary circumstances usually ejected by ciliary motion of the epithelium long before this. Therefore specially favorable moments must come to make their establishment possible. These are certainly brought about by many conditions. Nevertheless, the most important and most frequent helps for the establishment of the infection appear to be furnished by such diseases as, for example the measles, for a time rob the mucous membrane of respiration of its protecting epithelium, or which furnish stagnating secretions in which the tuberculous bacilli can establish themselves. Also, and that correctly, attention has been called to the fact, that by adhesions of the lungs and imperfect form of the thorax, which hinder a sufficient movement of the lungs and which are especially adapted to cause circumscribed collections of bronchial secretions, the arising of tuberculosis, that is the establishment of the tuberculous bacilli, is favored. If one makes clear to himself the necessity of such favorable moments for the entrance of the tuberculous bacilli, then it can no longer appear so striking that many persons, in spite of constant association with consumptives, are not infected, while others are plainly infected at the first opportunity, and still others after they have been exposed to the infection for a long time finally, nevertheless, fall a victim to the same. In the case of the first mentioned nothing helped the tuberculous bacilli, which were doubtless often enough inhaled, and they were therefore removed again from the respiratory passages ; the second had from the beginning a defective spot in their respiratory organs, on which the bacilli were able to fasten themselves, and it was only necessary that the infectious germ should reach just this spot ; the last mentioned not until later had such a defect and lost by means of it to a certain extent their immunity from tuberculosis. The difficulties which stand in the way of the establishment of the tuberculous bacilli in the upper air passages are greater and this fact explains the rare cases in which they primarily become diseased.

Since by far the greatest number of cases of tuberculosis begin in the lungs, it is to be supposed that the infection in all these cases has taken place in the manner just suggested by the inhalation of phthisic sputum dried and made into dust. On account of the immence production of the infectious material and on account of the frequent contact in which it must come with other parts of the human body, it is nevertheless not improbable that the infection can take place from other parts than the lungs. So I would say, that the primary attacks of lymph glands lying on the surface arising from scratches, skin-eruptions, etc., into which tuberculous bacilli have accidentally entered, have formed the entrance gate for the infection, from whence the bacilli have been carried farther and have got into the lymph glands, then when the original point of infection has been healed, it appears as if the disease-process had developed primarily in the glands. A number of cases in which in otherwise healthy human beings caseous lymph glands containing tuberculous bacilli were cut out from the back of the neck, I could not otherwise explain, than that they arose through infection from scratches on the skin of the head. Since the excrement of consumptives not rarely contains tuberculous bacilli, the same is true in regard to the danger of infection from this as from the sputum, when there is opportunity for its drying and being scattered as dust. But this does not occur probably very often ; all the same this possibility of spreading the infectious material is to be kept in view.

The second principal source for the tuberculous bacilli, namely, tuberculosis of the domestic animals, appears not to have anything like the importance of the phthisic sputum. The animals, as is well known, produce no sputum, so that during their life no tuberculous bacilli get from them into the outer world by means of the respiratory passages. Also in the excrement of tuberculous animals tuberculous bacilli appear to be only exceptionally present. On the contrary, it is a fact that the milk of tuberculous animals can cause infection. With the exception of this one way, therefore, the tuberculous virus can only have effect after the death of the animal and can only cause infection by the eating of the meat. Aside from the probably only rarely occurring cases of direct infection, which can follow from coming in contact with tuberculous parts of the flesh of little wounds and exoriations of the skin, the reception of the infectious material will result in this case only by means of the organs of digestion, and in accordance with this the first appearances of the disease must first show themselves here. But now primary tuberculosis of the intestines is not at all frequent in proportion to primary lung-tuberculosis—indeed, a decidedly rare affection. From this it is to be concluded, that the infection in question does not often occur from eating the flesh of tuberculous animals. Probably it would occur frequently if the visibly diseased parts of the flesh were not put aside, as is usually the case, and if, as is almost invariably the case, the meat were not eaten cooked. Also especially it must be considered that the tuberculosis eatable animals, especially the perlsucht of cattle, remains more or less localized, so that after all only the use of the tuberculously altered lungs, glands, etc., would be dangerous. That, nevertheless, the infection from the intestinal canal is indeed possible, is proved by the frequent cases of secondary intestinal tuberculosis of consumptives. which must be attributed to the swallowing of their own sputa. It is, to be sure, strange that, although it is to be supposed, that every consumptive swallows more or less of the tuberculous bacilli-bearing secretion from his lungs, nevertheless intestinal abscesses are not to be found in all. I explain this in the following manner : In the first place, the intestines appear to offer a still more unfavorable point of attack for the slowly growing tuberculous bacilli than the lungs. But further, the feeding-attempts with anthrax bacilli and their spores, have taught that anthrax bacilli, which contain no spores, are destroyed in the stomach, while the spores of these bacilli are able to pass through the stomach unharmed. On that account only spore-bearing substances can cause infection from the intestinal canal. The tuberculous bacilli will conduct themselves most probably in this regard, like the anthrax-bacilli, and only in case they are provided with spores will cause tuberculosis of the intestines, provided they do not go through the intestinal canal too quickly to render their germinating and establishing themselves at any point of the mucous membrane of the intestines possible. Just the same holds, of course, for the danger of an infection from tuberculous meat, and this circumstance may explain the relatively rare infection from the use of such meat.

The same conditions hold for infection from the milk of cows suffering from perlsucht. Before all things, if infection is to take place it is necessary that the milk contain tuberculous bacilli. But this appears only to be the case when the milk-glands themselves are tuberculously diseased. But since perlsucht-knots do not often occur in the udder, the milk of perlsucht cows will often possess no infectious properties. This explains immediately the contradictions in the statements of the various authors, who have made feeding attempts with milk from cows suffering from perlsucht. The one set maintain that they have gained positive results, and their statements are of such a sort that it is impossible to doubt the correctness of their observations. The others, on the contrary, could obtain no infection in the animals experimented with. This result is also correct. The positive results were then obtained from milk which accidentally contained tuberculous bacilli, the negative with milk which was free from bacilli.

If infection from tuberculous domestic animals in general does not appear to be frequent, it must by no means be under-rated. Perlsucht of cattle and the caseous changes in the lymph-glands of pigs are of so frequent occurrence that they deserve close attention. If, now, we follow the tuberculous bacilli which have got into the lungs by inhalation, into the skin by wounds, into the intestinal canal by swallowing, in their further conduct in the body, we see that they often remain for a long time—sometimes even permanently—in the place of their first establishment. From herds of epithelioid cells they form little knots which enclose giant cells, and regularly from the centre out, fall victims to coagulation-necrosis. The appearances which are conditioned upon the gradual growth of such a herd, and the regressive changes which always keep step with it, have been described in detail in a former section. The first sign of the spreading of the tuberculous process into the neighboring regions is the formation of similar knots in the neighborhood of the primary herd. The way, also, in which the migration of the bacilli from the first herd to the place where the secondary knots arise, is to be conceived, I have also already suggested. The following appears to me to be the simplest explanation of this proceeding. The tuberculous bacilli, since they possess no motion of their own, can only be moved along by elements possessing the power of motion, or by currents of liquid. But since the tuberculous knots have no vasal and one cannot see how other liquids, which are in motion, can get into the tuberculous herd and sweep away bacilli from them, nothing remains but the wandering cells, which according to experience, act the same part in other disease-producing bacteria, which those elements perform, that provide for the transport of the bacilli. The cell, laden with a bacillus only goes on until, under the influence of the parasite, it loses its power of motion. On the spot where the cell came to a stand-still, a new tuberculous knot must arise. In this manner groups of tubercles form, which melt, perish and cause destruction in the well-known manner.

With the supposition that the wandering cells may be the bearers of the bacilli, we see in the most natural manner the connection with the farther excursions which the tuberculous bacilli make in the body in almost all cases. When the wandering cell moves in the tissue-passages and must rely on its own power of motion, then the distance which it travels is only a short one and the newly arising infectious herd must lie in the neighborhood of the point of departure. But as soon as the wandering cells move in the lymph-vessels and the lymph-stream comes to their help in their movement, then they travel greater distances, as is seen not seldom in the tubercles spreading themselves out in the course of the lymph-vessels. But very often then the tuberculous bacilli are swept away still farther in the lymph-vessels and led into the nearest lymph-glands, where in like manner as in the first place of infection they call forth the formation of knots and caseous degeneration. The changes conditioned upon this in the gland-tissue appear usually to hinder a further progress of the bacilli by the way of lymph-passages. But by this no insurmountable barrier is placed in the way of the progress of the bacilli. They can, under special conditions, get into the stream of the blood. This happens when, as Ponfick has shown, the tuberculosis attacks the thoracic duct, and reaches the interior of the same ; the tuberculous bacilli are then led direct from the lymph-stream into the blood-stream.

A second, and moreover the most frequent cause for the entrance of tuberculous bacilli into the blood, has been discovered by Weigert. This is the formation of tuberculous knots in the walls of veins and the breaking through of the perishing knots into the lumen of the vasa.

A third possibility is suggested in the case described in the earlier pages of this paper, in which the bacilli grew into the lumen of an artery. In all these cases the bacilli were rapidly swept away by the blood-stream, scattered into the most various organs of the body and there established. If very many bacilli at one time got into the blood, then the conditions are exactly the same as in the experiment with the rabbit into whose ear-veins considerable quantities of tuberculous bacilli from a pure culture were injected. As well in the artificial as in the natural experiment, and in the same manner, tuberculous knots arise in great numbers, and moreover especially in the lungs, spleen and liver. Why these organs are so specially favored demands explanation. The connection between the localized tuberculous processes and the acute miliary tuberculosis which formerly appeared so enigmatical, and on that account has been characterized by many as impossible, has been made clear with unquestionable certainty by the discoveries of Ponfick and Weigert. This example of the manifold forms of a disease warns us forcibly against considering pathological changes, and especially infectious diseases only from an anatomical point of view unless forced to do so, but first of all to consider the ætiological relations as authoritative.

A considerable number of tuberculous bacilli do not always force themselves at once into the blood-passages. It can also occur that only comparatively a few bacilli are carried along by the blood-stream. Then there arise correspondingly fewer tuberculous herds, but which reach greater dimensions because in this case life is longer preserved, than when an immense eruption of tuberculous knots cause rapid death. Also in this matter the infection taking place in the natural way conducts itself just like that artificially generated. Sometimes only a very few bacilli get into the blood and only individual tubercles are formed, which then in course of time grow to considerable dimensions. This proceeding, which can repeat itself with intervening pauses, has been characterized by Weigert very fittingly as chronic miliary tuberculosis, in contrast to the acute, which, owing to the immense production of tubercles is quickly fatal.

To these last mentioned forms of miliary tuberculosis are joined those processes where, in certain places of the body, which are not easily suceptible to an invasion from without and apparently without a herd causing the infection, a tuberculosis confined to the spot is developed. This sort of process, among which the fungous carious infections are to be reckoned, arise strictly localized. One can scarcely explain their occurrence otherwise than that a single infectious germ, therefore a single bacillus, was deposited by the blood on the spot in question. But how is a single bacillus to get into the blood? Could it after being inhaled into the lungs get into the lung capillaries without previously causing in the lung itself a tuberculous herd? Such a supposition has to me little probability. The almost regular appearance of caseous or calcareous bronchial glands in the diseased conditions mentioned rather makes the supposition probable, that the lymph-glands are not always an unconquerable hindrance to the further progress of the bacilli, and that individual bacilli just as they are carried along by the wandering cells and the lymph-stream, can also by help of the wandering cells leave the lymph-glands in centripetal direction again and by the lymph-stream be carried into the blood. I do not doubt that, as in almost every case of miliary tuberculosis, the point of departure for the infection can be shown, one can also succeed in all cases of localized tuberculosis of the inner organs, as well as of the bones and joints, when they are dissected to find some older tuberculous herd, mostly perhaps caseous bronchial glands, from which single bacilli could get into the blood It is very probable also, that tuberculous bacillar meningitis of children in so far belongs here, as that in the same, although lungs, liver and spleen are very often free from tuberculosis, the bronchial glands are almost regularly found caseous, whence we may conclude that these latter in this case too are to be considered as the primary disease-herd. To be sure it is peculiar, that in this form of tubercul sis, in which plainly not single but numerous tuberculous bacilli are deposited by the blood, the pia mater is so favored a place of deposit.

If, as has already been shown in former parts of this work, the various forms of tuberculosis must be declared identical on account of the same qualities of the bacilli occurring in them and the cultures gained from these, as well as on account of the identity of the inoculating products proceeding from them, the progressive knowledge of their mode of originating gives new proofs of this supposition. At first sight, however different the forms of lung-phthisis, acute and chronic miliary tuberculosis, the affections of the glands and mucous membrane under the general figure of scrofula, tuberculosis of the bones and joints, of localized tuberculosis of single organs, as for example the kidneys and the intestines, may appear, we shall see without difficulty that they belong together when we look at their mode of formation. Only lupus offers in so far a certain difficulty in the identification with tuberculosis, as clinic observation state a distinction that cannot be overlooked in the conduct of lupus and undeniably tuberculous affections of the skin and mucous membrane. Nevertheless the ætiological reasons for the unity of these two diseases are too weighty to retire before this difference, which possibly may find its explanation in the individual disposition.

The relation is similar between the tuberculosis of animals, above all of perlsucht and tuberculosis in man. These also must on account of the identity of the parasites on which they are conditioned, be held to be identical with human tuberculosis in spite of the differences in the anatomical behavior and in their clinical course. It has, to be sure, been stated, especially with reference to perlsucht, that the transmission of this disease to man has not yet been certainly proved. On the other hand the following may be said : On account of the very slow development of the disease, the place and time of the infection and therewith the source of the same can no longer be confidently stated, when the first plain symptoms appear. On this account in the frequent inhalation-tuberculosis the mode of infection can be determined in a scientific manner only in comparatively few cases. Still less will this be possible in the much rarer cases of intestinal tuberculosis arising from the use of flesh or milk of cattle suffering from perlsucht, because here the uncertainty is heightened by the easily possible confusion with other much more frequent kinds of infection. It is therefore very questionable whether ever a case of human tuberculosis can without criticism be attributed to the use of the meat or milk of tuberculous animals. But if one thinks, that to the most various sorts of animals (cats, rabbits, guinea pigs, field mice) by inoculation with masses of perlsucht and the pure cultures gained from them, a disease can be generated with the greatest regularity which anatomically is exactly like the disease caused by inoculation with tuberculous masses, and which kills the animals with the same certainty as the last, then it is not to be expected that man should be an exception to this disease-poison. If in the course of further investigations again a difference between the perlsucht and the tuberculous bacilli should show itself, which would compel us to consider the same as only near relations, we should even then have all cause to hold the perlsucht bacilli as suspicious in the highest degree. From the hygienic standpoint the same measures must be taken against it as against the infection through tuberculous bacilli, so long as it is not proved that man can bring perlsucht bacilli in co - tact with skin-wounds without danger, that he can inhale the same or bring their spores into his intestinal canal without becoming tuberculous.

The considerable variety in the course of the disease in various individuals of the same species, and in their sensitiveness to the tuberculous virus, appears to speak against a common classification of all the disease-forms conditioned by tuberculous bacilli. These are nevertheless appearances which reappear in more or less marked a manner. One helps himself in this case by supposing a different disposition for the disease, as well as what concerns the attack of the same and its more or less intense course, without that an explanation of the same is given by this characterizing of the appearance. A number of such differences in the form of tuberculosis is already simply explained by the difference of the point of infection. Then the quantity of the infectious material originally taking effect seems to be of essential importance. Single infectious germs are held within bonds more easily and for a longer time by the organism on account of their slower development, so that they remain localized ; while, when many germs are imported at once, they support each other in their work of destruction. A definite representation of that which is characterized as individual disposition one can make for all conditions, in which according to our previous supposition, certain favorable moments, such as are afforded by defects in the epithelial covering of the respiratory mucous membrane, stagnating secretions, disturbances of respiration, etc., aid the establishment of the tuberculous bacilli.

If then a large number of the appearances combined under the expression disposition may be referred to simple and easily explainable relations, there nevertheless remain some facts hard to explain, or not to be explained, which compel us to allow the supposition of a disposition to exist for the present. This is above all the striking difference of tuberculosis in its course in children and in grown people ; further, the undeniable predisposition of many families for tuberculosis. In the last case many cases of tuberculosis laid at the door of this predisposition might much better be referred to the increased opportunity of infection. One can also think of special predisposing causes belonging to the family character, such as inclination to catarrh of the respiratory organs, defective structure of the thorax. Nevertheless there are many observations relative to this point which do not admit of such explanations. Moreover,

single cases of the disease have already often taught that one and the same
person is not at every time an equally favorable subject for the development
of the parasites, for, as is well known, it occurs not rarely that tuberculous
herds which had reached no slight extent, shrivel, make scars and heal.   That
is as much as to say that the same body which, at the invasion of the tuberculous
bacilli gave a favorable breeding-ground for the same, so that they could increase
and spread, gradually loses these favorable properties, changes itself into a bad
breeding-ground and so sets a boundary to the further growth of the bacilli.
There existed, therefore, in the same person at one time a disposition for tuberculosis and at another time not.   Wherein this distinction is founded,
whether in a change in the chemical composition of the juices of the tissue,
or in physical conditions, that must be taught by later investigations.   So much
is certain, that such differences exist and there is certainly nothing against the
supposition that similar conditions, favorable or unfavorable to the tuberculous
bacilli, may exist in certain persons not only for a time, but also during the
entire life.

What still concerns the much discussed question of hereditary tuberculosis,
after what has just been said, I can express in a few words.   No facts exist
which justify the supposition that intra-uterine or extra-uterine tuberculous
bacilli can be present in the organism of a child, without bringing about visible
changes in a comparatively short time.   But until now tuberculosis has been
very seldom found in the fœtus or in the newly born child, and we may, therefore, conclude that the infectious material has effect only exceptionally during
the intra-uterine life.   This supposition is confirmed by the fact that of my
experimental animals, especially guinea pigs, which not seldom were pregnant
before or after the tuberculous infection, none have borne young which were
tuberculous at birth.   The young coming from mothers tuberculous to a high
degree were free from tuberculosis and remained healthy for months.   In my
opinion hereditary tuberculosis finds its most natural explanation, if it be supposed that not the infectious germ itself, but certain qualities favoring the
development of the germs coming into contact with the body at a later period,
therefore, that which we call disposition, be inherited.

The ætiology of tuberculosis, as it was here developed on the foundation
of our knowledge of the tuberculous bacillus in detail, scarcely offers anything
new.   Cohnheim had represented tuberculosis as an infectious disease and described its ætiology correspondingly before the discovery of the tuberculous
bacillus.   In this direction, therefore, my investigations have brought no essential progress to science, and yet it must be considered as a gain that upon the
very important question of the infectious nature of tuberculosis, which until
then had been disputed by most, now such proofs are furnished as to admit
of no reasonable objections.   Not less important is it, that the tuberculous
bacilli give a sure test of what in the future shall be considered as belonging
to the territory of tuberculosis.   The diagnosis of tuberculosis will in doubtful
cases be made dependent upon the proof of tuberculous bacilli.   Practice has, as
is well known, made use of this aid to a great extent and moreover with complete success, and has thereby furnished a rich material for proving the correctness of my opinion of the importance of tuberculous bacilli.   Already from

this an appreciable advantage has resulted in the discovery of the tuberculous bacillus. But it is to be hoped, that also in other respects something may be gained by it, which can be made useful in fighting the disease. After the experiments already undertaken no great outlook appears to exist in a therapeutic direction, of finding successful means of influencing the parasites in the body of the patient. I would lay so much more value upon the prophylactic measures. These must partly be directed to directly destroying the tuberculous bacilli by suitable methods of disinfection, partly they must strive to preserve the healthy from contact with the tuberculous bacilli in all those conditions in which a reliable destruction of the parasites is not possible.

It appears to me not to be too early to proceed against tuberculosis with prophylactic measures. But owing to the great spread of this disease, all steps which are taken against the same will have to reckon with the social condition, and, therefore, it must be carefully considered in what way and how far one may go on this road without prejudicing the advantages gained, by unavoidable disturbances and other disadvantages. It would lead too far to go into a detailed discussion of the prophylaxis in this place, and I reserve my views in regard to it for another opportunity.

CATALOGUE.

*Allen's American Cattle. Their History, Breeding and Management. By [Lewis F. Allen. Illustrated. 12mo, cloth.. 2 50

*Allen's Domestic Animals. A History and Description of the Horse, Mule, Cattle, Sheep, Swine, Poultry, and Farm Dog, with directions for breeding, treatment, &c. By R. I. Allen. 12mo, cloth............................ 1 00

**American Veterinary Review. A monthly journal of Veterinary Medicine and Surgery, entirely devoted to the interests of the veterinary profession and the only monthly journal of the kind published in the United States. Subscription per year *net* post paid $3.00. Single copies *net*. 25

Anderson and Waring. "The Saddle Horse." A complete guide to the riding and training of saddle horses by E. L. Anderson and George E. Waring. 12mo, cloth, illustrated.. 1 00

*Armatage. "Every Man His Own Horse Doctor." In which is embodied Blaine's "Veterinary Art," with 330 original illustrations, colored plates. anatomical drawings, &c. 8vo, half leather................................. 7 50

*Armatage. "Every Man His Own Cattle Doctor." In which is embodied Blaine's Veterinary Art," with 330 original illustrations, colored plates, anatomical Drawing, &c. 8vo, half leather................................. 7 50

*Ashmont. Principles of Dog Training. 12mo, cloth...... 50

*Ashmont. On Dogs, their Management and Treatment in Disease. 12mo, cloth............................ 2 00

Banham. Posological Tables for Veterinary Students and Practitioners. By George A. Banham, F.R.C.V.S. Cloth. (Just published.).................................... 1 00

*Battersby. "The Bridle Bits." A valuable little work on Horsemanship. By Col. J. C. Battersby. 12mo, cloth.... 1 00

*Baucher. New Method of Horsemanship. Including the Breaking and Training of Horses...................... 1 00

* **Billings.** " The Relation of Animal Diseases to the Public
Health and their Prevention." By Frank S. Billings, D.V.S.
8vo, cloth 4 00

*Cattle.** Their Varieties and Management in Health and Disease
12 mo, Boards.................................... 60

* **Chauveau.** The Comparative Anatomy of the Domesticated
Animals. By A. Chauveau, Professor at Lyons Veterinary
School, France. New edition, translated, enlarged and revised.
By George Fleming, F. R. C. V. S. 8vo, cloth, with 450
illustrations.. 6 00

* **Chawner.** Diseases of the Horse, and How to Treat Them.
A Manual of Special Pathology for the use of Horsemen,
Farmers and Students. By Robert Chawner. 12mo, cloth,
illustrated... 1 25

* **Clarke.** " Horses' Teeth." A Treatise on their Mode of
Development, Physiological Relations, Anatomy, Pathology,
Dentistry, etc. Revised and enlarged. By W. H. Clarke.
12mo, cloth 2 00

*Coburn's " **Swine Husbandry.**" Manual for the Rearing
Breeding and Management of Swine. By F. D. Coburn,
Cloth, illustrated...... .... 1 75

Courtney. Manual of Veterinary Medicine and Surgery. By
Edward Courtney, V.S. Crown, 8vo, cloth (new)........ 3 50

*Dadd.** The American Cattle Doctor. A complete work on the
Diseases of Cattle, Sheep and Swine. By Geo. H. Dadd,
"M.D.V.S. 12mo, $1.50. 8vo, illustrated............. 2 50

* **Dadd.** The American Reformed Horse Book. A treatise on the
Causes, Symptoms and Cure of every Disease incident to the
Horse. By G. H. Dadd, M. D., V. S. 8vo, cloth, illustrated 2 50

* **Dadd.** The Modern Horse Doctor. Containing Practical Observations on the Causes, Nature and Treatment of Diseases in
Horses. By G. H. Dadd, M. D., V. S. 12mo, cloth, illus. 1 50

Dalziel. " British Dogs "—Their Varieties, History, Characteristics, Breeding, Management and Exhibition. Illustrated with full page portraits. 12mo, cloth............ 4 00

Dalziel. " The Diseases of Dogs," their Pathology, Diagnosis
and Treatment, with a dictionary of Canine Materia-Medica.
By Hugh Dalziel. 12mo, cloth..... .... 1 00
Paper...................... 60

Dana. "Tables in Comparative Physiology," giving Comparative weight, temperature, circulation of the blood, respiration, digestion, nervous force and action between man and the lower animals and birds, by Prof. C. L. Dana, M.D. Chart on paper...... .... $0 25

Day. The Race-horse in Training, with some hints on Racing and Racing Reform. By Wm. Day. Demy, 8vo....... 3 60

*Du Hays, on the Percheron Horse. Translated from the French of Charles Du Hays. 12mo, cloth, illustrated.. 1 00

Dun. Veterinary Medicines, Their Actions and Uses. By Finley Dun, V. S. New American edition from the latest English one. 8vo, cloth............................ 3 50
New Revised English edition, 8vo, cloth................ 5 00

Orders for either edition of this work should specify which one is wanted.

Fearnley. Lecture on the Examination of Horses as to Soundness, Sale and Warranty. By W. Fearnley, M. R. C. V. S. 12 mo, cloth.......... .... $3 00

Fearnley. Lessons in Horse Judging, and on the Summering of Hunters. 12mo, cloth, illustrated............... 1 60

Fleming. "Roaring in Horses." (Laryngismus Paralyheus). His History, Nature, Causes, Prevention, and Treatment. 8vo, cloth............................. 2 00

Fleming. "Animal Plagues." Their History, Nature, and Prevention, by George Fleming, F.R.C.V.S., etc., being a chronolgical history from the earliest times to 1844 *First Series,* comprising a history of Animal Plagues from B. C., 1490 to A. D. 1800. 8vo, cloth.... .... 6 00
Second Series, containing the history from A. D., 1800, to A. D., 1844. 8vo, cloth............................. 4 80

Fleming (George). Practical Horse-keeper. By Dr. George Fleming, F.R.C.V.S. 12mo, cloth.................... 2 00

Fleming. "Actinomykosis," a new, infectious Disease of Man and Animals by George Fleming, F.R.C.V.S. Paper. 40

Fleming. A Treatise on Practical Horseshoeing. By George Fleming, M. R. C. V. S. Cloth................ 75

Fleming. "Human and Animal Variolœ," a study in comparative pathology. Paper........................ 40

Fleming. "Operative Veterinary Surgery." Part I. By Dr. George Fleming, M.R.C.V.S. This valuable work, the most practical treatise yet issued on the subject in the English language, is devoted to the common operations of Veterinary Surgery; and the concise descriptions and directions of the text are illustrated with numerous wood engravings. 8vo, cloth... 3 50

Fleming. "Propagation of Tuberculosis.", Being the influence of Heredity and Contagion on the Propagation of Tuberculosis, and the Injurious Effects from the Consumption of the Flesh and Milk of Tuberculous Animals. By George Fleming, M.D., M.R.C.V.S., Herr Lydtin, and Dr. Van Hertsen, being their joint report on the subject before the Veterinary Congress held at Brussels in September, 1883. 8vo, cloth... 2 25

Fleming's Rabies and Hydrophobia. History, Natural Causes, Symptoms and Prevention. By George Fleming, M.R.C.V.S. 8vo, cloth......................... 6 00

Fleming. Veterinary Obstetrics. Including the Accidents and Diseases incident to Pregnancy, Parturition, and the Early Age in Domesticated Animals. By Geo. Fleming, F.R.C.V.S. With 212 illustrations. 8vo, cloth.................... 6 00

***The Dog.** By Dinks, Mathew and Hutchinson. Compiled and Edited by Frank Forester. Containing full instructions in all that relates to Breeding, Rearing, Breaking, Feeding, Training, Kenneling, and Conditioning of Dogs, with valuable recipes for the Treatment of all Diseases. Cloth, 8vo..................................... 3 00

Fleming. "The Contagious Diseases of Animals," their influence on the wealth and health of nations. 12mo, paper, 25

***Floyd.** Hints on Dog Breaking. A clear, concise and practical hand book. 12mo............................... 50

***Fowler.** "Jersey, Alderney and Guernsey Cows." Their History, Nature and Management. Edited from numerous writers, by W. P. Hazard. 8vo, cloth, with illustrations... 1 50

Gleason. How to Handle and Educate Vicious Horses, by Oscar R. Gleason. 12 mo, cloth..................... 50

Gresswell. "Manual of the Theory and Practice of Equine Medicine." By J. B. Gresswell, M.R.C.V.S., and Albert Gresswell, M.R.C.V.S. 8 vo. cloth 3 50

Gresswell. The Equine Hospital Prescriber; drawn up for the use of Veterinary Practitioners and Students. By Drs. James B. and Albert Gresswell, M.R.C.V.S. Cloth......   1 00

Gresswell. Veterinary Pharmacology and Therapeutics, by James B. Gresswell, M.R.C.V.S. 16 mo, cloth (new)....   1 50

Gresswell. Veterinary Pharmacopæia, Materia Medica and Therapeutics. By George and Charles Gresswell, M.R.C.V.S., with descriptions and physiological actions of medicines, by Albert Gresswell. Crown, 8vo, cloth...... ....   3 50

Gresswell. The Bovine Prescriber for the use of Veterinary and Veterinary Students. By James B. and Albert Gresswell, M.R.C.V.S. 16mo, cloth............................   1 00

Guenon. Treatise on Milch Cows........................   1 00

Harris. *On the Pig,* By Joseph Harris. 12mo, **cloth.....**   1 50

Hayes. Veterinary Notes for Horses Owners. An Every-day Horse Book. Illustrated, By M. Hayes. 12mo, cloth.   5 00

Hazard. The Jersey, Alderney and Guernsey Cow. Cloth...   1 50

Healtley. Practical Veterinarian Remedies. By G. S. Heatley, M.R.C.V.S. 12mo, cloth...............................   1 00

Heatley. Our Dogs and their Diseases. By G. S. Heatley, M.R.C.V.S. 12mo, cloth............................   1 25

*Heatley. Every Man his own Veterinary. 12mo, cloth...   2 50

*Herbert. Hints to Horse Keepers. A Complete Manual for Horse Men. By H. W. Herbert (Frank [Forester)- 12mo, illustrated......................... ....   1 75

Hill. The Management and Diseases of the Dog. Containing full instructions for Breeding, Rearing and Kenneling Dogs. Their different Diseases, embracing Distemper, Mouth, Teeth, Tongue, Gullet, Respiratory Organs, Hepatitis, Indigestions, Gastritis, St. Vitus' Dance, Bowel Diseases, Paralysis, Rheumatism, Fits, Rabies, Skin Diseases, Canker, Diseases of the Limbs, Fractures, Operations, etc. How to detect and how to cure them. Their Medicines, and the doses in which they can be safely administered. By J. Woodroffe Hill, F. R. C. V. S. 12mo, cloth, extra, fully illustrated   2 00

Hill. "The Principles and Practice of Bovine Medicine and Surgery," by J. Woodroffe Hill, F.R.C.V.S. # This is undoubtedly the most comprehensive work on the subject of cattle and their diseases. The book, while of a thoroughly standard character, is yet written so that non-professionals may obtain a practical knowledge of the diseases attending the bovine stock, and the most intelligent method of treating them.

The scope of the work comprises an introductory chapter on "Health and Disease;" a chapter on "Diseases of the Heart and its Membranes;" one, "Diseases of the Respiratory Organs; "Diseases and Injuries of the Blood Vessels;" Dentition, Diseases of the Teeth, Jaws, Tongue and Mouth; of the Stomach; of the Bowels; of the Liver and Spleen; of the Urinary Organs; of the Generative Organs; Anatomy and Physiology of the Cow; Parturition; Diseases of the Fœtus; Monstrosities; Diseases and Abnormalities of the Young Animal; Diseases immediately connected with Parturition; Diseases and Abnormalities of the Mammary Gland and Teats; Diseases of the Nervous System; of the Eye and Appendages; of the Ear; of the Skin; Internal Parasites, Blood and General Diseases; Accidents and Operations; Poison and Antidotes.

Octavo, 664 Pages, with 153 illustrations on wood and 19 full page colored plates. Cloth...............................$10 00

Hanover. Practical Treatise on the Law of Horses. Law of Bargains and Sale and Warranty of Horses and other Live Stock. The Rules as to Unsoundness and Vice, etc., etc. By M. D. Hanover. 8vo, sheep....................... 4 00

*Holcombe. "Laminitis." A Contribution to Veterinary Pathology. By A. A. Holcombe, V. S. Pamphlet.... ... 50

*Howden. "How to Buy and Sell the Horse." The object of this book is to explain in the simplest manner what constitutes a sound horse from an unsound one. 12mo, cloth, 1 00

Hutchinson. "Dog Breaking." An Easy, Expeditious and Certain Method. By Gen. W. N. Hutchinson. 8vo, cloth.. 3 00

Jennings. Horse Training Made Easy. A Practical System of Educating the Horse. By Robert Jennings, V. S. 12mo, cloth. 1 25

Jennings. Swine, Sheep and Poultry. Embracing a History and Varieties of each ; Breeding, Management, Disease, etc. By Robert Jennings, V. S. 12mo, cloth................ $1 25

Jennings. Cattle and their Diseases ; with the best Remedies adapted to their Cure. By Robert Jennings, V. S. 12mo, cloth.. 1 25

Jennings, On the Horse and **his Diseases.** By Robert Jennings, V. S. 12mo, cloth........................... 1 25

Journal of Comparative Medicine and Surgery. A Quarterly Journal devoted to the Diseases of Animals, particularly of the Horse. Published in January, April, July and October. Subscriptions (net) $2.00 per annum. Single copies, post paid (net)........................ 60

Lambert. "The Germ Theory of Disease." Bearing upon the health and welfare of man and the domesticated animals. By James Lambert, F.R.C.V.S 8vo, paper............ 40

Law. Farmers' Veterinary Adviser. A Guide to the Prevention and Treatment of Disease in Domestic Animals. By James Law, Professor of Veterinary Medicine in Cornell University. Illustrated. 8vo, cloth...................... 3 00

Law. The Lung Plague of Cattle ; Contagious Pleuro-Pneumonia. Illustrated. By James Law, Professor of Veterinary Medicine in Cornell University. Paper, 100 pages........ 30
American edition................................. 1.50

Lehndorff. "Horse Breeding Recollections." By G. Lehndorff. Being the personal experiences of a breeder of English thoroughbreds, with pedigrees, plans, etc., etc. 8vo, cloth...................................... 4 20

*Liautard. "Animal Castration." A concise and practical Treatise on the Castration of the Domestic Animals ; the only work on the subject in the English language. Illustrated with forty-four cuts. 12mo, cloth..................... 2 00

Liautard. "How to Tell the Age of the Domestic Animals." By Dr. A. Liautard, H.M.R.C.V.S. Profusely illustrated. 12mo, cloth....................................... 50

Liautard. Chart of the Age of Domesticated Animals. By A. Liautard, M. D., V. S. Profusely illustrated, on a card 21½ by 28½ inches............................. 50

Liautard. Vade Mecum of Equine Anatomy. By A. Liautard, M. D., V. S., Professor of Comparative Anatomy at the American Veterinary College. An invaluable and comprehensive little work, especially adapted to Veterinary Students and Surgeons. Adopted in several of the Colleges as a text book, new edition, revised and enlarged. just published. 12mo, cloth.. 2 00

Liautard. Translation of "Zundel on the Horse Foot." Cloth. 2 00

Liautard. " On the Lameness of the Horse." By A. Liautard, M. D., V.S.. 2 50

Long. Book of the Pig. Its selection, Breeding, Feeding and Management. By James Long. Illustrated with full pages plates. Large Octavo, cloth................... 6 00

*Magner. "Art of Taming and Educating the Horse." By D. Magner. This is a great book, the result of years of labor and research by the author, who has spared no expense in its publication. In addition to the chapters on the education of the horse, there are others on the Feeding, Stabling, Shoeing, with directions for practical treatment for Sickness, Lameness, &c., &c. The book, which contains upwards of 1000 pages, is illustrated with 900 engravings expressly prepared for the book. It is a thick 8vo, cloth, (net)........ 5 00
    Sheep ...." 6 00
    Full Morocco...........................".......... 7 50

Mayhew. " Dogs and their Management." With illustrations depicting the Position of the Dog in Disease. 16mo, boards. 75

*Mayhew. " Horse Management." With remarks on His Anatomy, Medicine, Shoeing, Teeth, etc. With over 400 illustrations. 8vo, cloth............................. 3 00

Mayhew. " The Horse Doctor." An Accurate Account, with Prescriptions and Modes of Treatment of all Equine Diseases. By Edward Mayhew, M. R. C. V. S. To which is appended " Practical Horseshoeing," by George Fleming. With 400 illustrations. 8vo, cloth.................... 3 00

Meyrick. Stable Management and the Prevention of Diseases Among Horses in India, by J. J. Meyrick, F.R.C.V.S. 12mo. cloth............................. .... 1 00

McBride. Anatomical Outlines of the Horse. Revised and Enlarged by T. M. Mayer, M. R. C. V. S. With colored illustrations. 12mo, cloth................. .... 3 00

McClure. Diseases of American Horses, Cattle and Sheep. Their Treatment : with full description of the Medicines employed. By R. McClure, M. D., V. S. 12mo, cloth, illustrated..   1 25

McClure. American Gentlemen's Stable Guide ; with the most Approved Methods of Feeding, Grooming and Managing the Horse. By Robert McClure, M. D., V. S. 12mo, cloth... $1 00

M'Fadyean. "Anatomy of the Horse, a Dissection Guide." By J. M. McFadyean, M.R.C.V.S., and instructor in Anatomy at the Royal Veterinary College at Edinburgh. This book is intended for Veterinary students, and offers to them in its 48 full page colored plates, numerous other engravings and excellent text, the most valuable and practical aid in the study of Veterinary Anatomy, especially in the dissecting room. 8vo. cloth...   **6** 50

M'Fadyean. "Comparative Anatomy of the Domesticated Animals. By J. M'Fadyean, M.B., C.M. B.Sc., M.R.C.V.S. Profusely illustrated and to be issued in two parts Part I. —Osteology, now ready. 8vo, paper 2 50, cloth...   3 00

*Miles. Stock breeding. a practical treatise on the applications of the laws of Developement and Heredity, to the improvement and breeding of the Domestic Animals. By Manly Miles, M.D. 12mo, cloth.....   1 50

Moreton. "On Horsebreaking." By Robert Moreton. 12mo, cloth..   50

Navin. "The Explanatory Stock Doctor," for the use of the Farmer, Breeder and Owner of the Horse. With numerous illustrations. By John Nicholson Navin. V.S. 8vo. sheep..   4 75

*Percheron. Horse in America and France. Cloth.   1 00

*Powers. The American Merino for Wool or Mutton. By Stephen Powers. Cloth............................   1 50

*Randall. Fine Wool Sheep Husbandry. By H. R. Randall, LL.D. Giving prominent characteristics of different breeds, etc. 12mo, cloth............................   1 00

*Randall. Practical Shepherd. A Complete Treatise on the Breeding, Management and Disease of the Sheep. By H. R. Randall, LL.D. Cloth, illustrated..............   2 00

*Randall. Sheep Husbandry. A General Treatise on the Sheep. 8vo, cloth, illustrated............................   1 50

Reynolds. "Breeding and Management of Draught Horses," by Richard S. Reynolds. M.R.C.V.S. Crown, 8vo, cloth.   1 40

*Riley. The Mule. A Treatise on theBreeding, Training and
    Uses to which he may be put. 12mo, cloth, illustrated. ...   1 50

Robertson.. "The Practice of Equine Medicine." A texte-
    book, exhibiting in a concise form a detailed account of the
    the principle diseases to which the horse is liable, and the
    modes of management and treatment in accordance with
    what are known as the recognized general principles of
    medicine. Especially adapted for the use of Veterinary
    Students and Veterinarians. By W. Robertson, Principal
    and Professor of Hippopathology in the Royal Veterinary
    College, London. 8vo, cloth, 806 pages, revised edttion.   6 50

Russell. Scientific Horse Shoeing......................   3 00

Smith. Manual of Veterinary Hygiene. A new and valuable
    work on a most important branch of veterinary practice
    never before treated so exhaustively. Crown, 8vo, cloth..   3 50

*Stables. "Cats." Their Points and Classifications; with chap-
    ters an Feline Ailments, and their Remedies; How to Train
    them, etc. By Gordon Stables. M.D. Crown 8vo, illust..   2 00

*Stables. Dogs in their Relation to the Public—Social, Sanitary
    and Legal. By Gordon Stables, M.D............   75

* Stables. "Ladies' Dogs as Companions." By Gordon Stables.
    12mo, plates..   2 00

*Stables. "Our Friend the Dog." A complete Guide to the
    Points and Properties of all known Breeds, and to their suc-
    cessful management in Health and Disease. By Gordon
    Stables, M.D. Crown 8vo, cloth, with numerous illustra-
    tions................................ ....   3 00

*Stables. "The Practical Kennel Guide". With plain instruc-
    tions how to rear and breed dogs for pleasure, show, and
    profit. 12mo, illustrated 1 50

* Stonehenge. Every Horse Owner's Cyclopedia. The An-
    atomy and Physiology of the Horse. General Characteristics,
    Points, Principles of Breeding, Treatment of Brood Mares
    and Foal ; Raising and Breaking of the Colt ; Stables and
    Stable Management ; Riding, Driving, etc., etc.; Diseases
    and their Treatment ; Medicines, and how to Use Them ;
    Accidents, Fractures and Necessary Operations ; including,
    also, articles on the American Trotting Horse. 8vo, illus-
    trated with 2 engravings and 80 wood cuts. cloth......... $3 75
    Sheep...................................... .. ..   4 50
    Half Morocco. 5 50

Steele. "Diseases of the Dog." By J. H. Steele, V.S., author of the Diseases of the Ox. A text-book especially intended to furnish the Veterinary Practitioner the most recent methods of treating the diseases of the dog, illust., cloth..   3 50

*Steel. A treatise on the Diseases of the Ox, being a Manual of Bovine Pathology, especially adapted to Veterinary Practitioners and Students. By John Henry Steel, M.R.C.V.S, F.Z.S. *Containing:* Bovine Diseases, Therapeutics and Materia Medica, Diseases of the Circulatory System, Digestive System, Respiratory Apparatus, Urine and Urinary Apparatus, Organs of Special Sense, Nervous System, of the Skeleton, Generative Organs (Male and Female), Lactiferous Apparatus, Milk and its Diseases, Wounds and Surgical Conditions, Diseases of Young Animals, etc. One volume of over 500 pages, 8vo, with 118 illustrations, cloth............................   6 00

*Stonehenge, "On the Horse in the Stable and Field. On his Varieties, Management, Anatomy, Physiology, etc. Illustrated with 170 engravings.

English edition, 8vo, cloth 3 50
American edition,   " 2 00

*Stonehenge. The Dogs of Great Britain and other Countries, their Breeding. Training and Management. 100 illustrations   2 00

Strangeway. "Veterinary Anatomy." New edition, revised and edited by I. Vaughn, F.L.S., M.R.C.V.S., with several hundred illustrations. 8vo. cloth 7 50

Tellor. Diseases of "Live Stock," and their most Efficient Remedies. By Lloyd V. Tellor. 8vo, cloth, illustrated..   2 50
Sheep.......................................   3 00

*Veterinary Journal and Annals of **Comparative Pathology.** (English). Edited by Dr. George Fleming. A Monthly journal devoted to the interests of Veterinarians. Subscriptions received (including postage), per annum, net,   5 00
Sample or single copies.................(Net, postpaid),   50

Veterinary Diagrams. Five Charts, each 22x28 inches in size, on stout paper, as follows :

No. 1. With eight colored illustrations. External Form and Elementary Anatomy of the Horse...................   1 50
No. 2. Unsoundness and Defects of the Horse. With fifty wood-cuts.......................................   75
No. 3. The Age of the Domestic Animals. With forty-two wood-cuts......................................   75

No. 4. The Shoeing of the Horse, Mule, and Ox. With
fifty-nine wood-cuts..................................   75
   No. 5. The Elementary Anatomy, Points, and Butcher's
Joints of the Ox. With seventeen colored illustrations..... 1 50
   These are printed with explanatory text. Price per set of
five... 5 00

Walley. "Four Bovine S~ourges." (Pleuro-Pneumonia,
Foot and Mouth Disease, Cattle Plague and Tubercle.)
With an Appendix on the Inspection of Live Animals and
Meat. By Thomas Walley, M.R.C.V.S. With 49 colored
illustrations and numerous wood cuts. 4to, cloth. (Recently
published).. 6 40

* **Waring.** Riding and Training of Saddle Horses. 12mo,
cloth... 1 50

Williams. Principles and Practice of Veterinary Medicine.
New edition, entirely revised, and illustrated with numerous
plain and colored plates. By W. Williams, M. R. C. V. S.
8vo, cloth. American edition...............Reduced to 5 00
English edition.................................... 7 50
   In ordering, specify which edition is desired.

Williams. Principles and Practice of Veterinary Surgery.
New edition, entirely revised, and illustrated with numerous
plain and colored plates. By W. Williams, M. R. C. V. S.
8vo, cloth.............................Reduced to 7 50

* **Woodruff.** Trotting Horse in America ; how to Train and
Drive him ; with Reminiscences of the Turf. By Hiram
Woodruff. 12mo, cloth... .... 2 50

* **Youat and Martin on Cattle.** A Treatise on their Breeds.
Management and Diseases. 12mo, cloth............. 1 75

* **Youatt and Martin, on the Hog.** 12mo, cloth........ 1 00

* **Youatt and Spooner, on the Horse.** Its Structure, Diseases, and Remedies; Rules to Buyers, Breeders, Shoers, &c.
12mo, cloth illustrated.............................. 1 50

* **Youatt, on Sheep.** A General Treatise. 8vo, cloth........ 1 00

* **Youatt.** "The Horse." By W. Youatt. Together with a
Dissertation on the American Trotting Horse, and an Essay
on the Ass and Mule, by J. S. Skinner. 8vo, cloth........ 1 75

Zundel. "The Horse's Foot and its Diseases. By A. Zundel,
Principal Veterinarian of Alsace-Lorraine. Translated by Dr.
A. Liautard, V.S. 12mo, cloth. Illustrated 2 00